For anyone who's ever looked at an old building and wondered what it remembers.

This story wouldn't exist without the voices, faces, and stories of the North.

Thank you to those who've ever wandered the back lanes of Darwen and felt something stirring in the stonework.

Special thanks to those who encouraged, questioned, edited, or simply asked, "How's the book coming?"

You kept the thread going.

DARWEN'S ECHOES: THE MILL'S GRASP

by Miles Darby

CHAPTER ONE

The Unblinking Eye and
a Missing Rhythm

Arthur Pickering knew exactly when the number 1 bus turned onto Market Street—9:03 a.m. sharp. He didn't need the antique grandfather clock to confirm it—the familiar floorboard rumble told him all he needed to know.

His world, once sprawling and noisy with the rhythmic clatter of looms and the boisterous camaraderie of the mill floor, had shrunk. Now it was confined to these four walls, the worn armchair by the window, and the expansive pane of glass that framed his living room. Beyond it, Darwen town centre unfolded like a meticulously crafted diorama, a miniature world teeming with unwitting actors in a silent play. The distant silhouette of Darwen Tower, a stoic sentinel on the moors, loomed like a smudge against the perpetually bruised Lancashire sky—a constant reminder of the vastness he could no longer access.

Art, as everyone called him, was sixty-two, a former textile worker. His hands, once deft with thread and machinery, had been transformed by time and arthritis. Gnarled and stiff, his knuckles bulged like ancient tree roots. The doctor had been kind, if vague: Rest, Mr Pickering. Your joints need it. Your heart needs it.

Rest, Art had discovered, was a polite synonym for boredom—a slow, creeping rot that dulled the mind. Since his wife Eleanor passed five years ago, the silence in the flat had only deepened. Her gentle bustle. Her baking. Her radio, always slightly off-tune—

all gone. What remained was the rustle of his newspaper, the low hum of the telly, and the tick of that bloody clock.

So, he watched.

He had a pair of battered binoculars—relics from a brief bird-watching phase Eleanor had dragged him into years ago. Now, they served a new purpose: urban safari. From his window perch, the world came alive in magnified detail. He knew the routines of the town better than most. Faces, patterns, the choreography of ordinary lives—all etched into his mind.

There was Mrs Henderson, the Loaf Lady, who always bought two loaves at 9:05 sharp, her pink shopping trolley squeaking like clockwork. There was young Gary, the Whistler, Darwen's most tone-deaf postman, who delivered with unwavering cheer. And Lamppost Larry, a scruffy terrier whose loyalty to one particular lamppost never wavered.

But none fascinated Art quite like the lad with the rucksack.

He didn't know his name, but he knew everything else. Early twenties, always in motion despite a faint limp. The lad's bright orange-and-blue rucksack and neon-green headphones made him impossible to miss. He moved with precision, passing the Town Hall, then the fish and chip shop—the scent of cod and chips clinging to the air—before slowing, always, outside the antique shop: Finch's Curios.

Finch's Curios sat oddly between a garish vape shop and a cluttered charity shop—like a relic resisting the pull of modernity. It was an unlikely island of stillness on a busy stretch. The windows, though never gleaming, bore the marks of age more than neglect—like memories you'd rather forget. Inside, Art had spied all manner of cast-offs: porcelain dolls with dead eyes, heavy furniture, dull silver. Finch himself—a grey, owl-like man in his late fifties—opened the shop at 9:00 a.m. daily, wiping the glass with a care that bordered on reverence. Always the same movements. Always the same glass. Methodical. Ritualistic.

This particular Monday, the lad's ritual unfolded as usual. He slowed outside the shop, eyes fixed on something in the cluttered window.

Art adjusted the binoculars, zooming in. A small, polished wooden box sat front and centre—darker than Finch's usual stock. It gleamed oddly, untouched by the layer of dust clinging to everything else. Out of place, Art thought. Too pristine. He remembered the recent break-in at Darwen Museum—several Victorian pieces stolen, including a music box. If Finch had it, he certainly wouldn't have it on display. Not something like that.

The lad hesitated. Then pushed open the door.

The bell above the shop gave its usual soft, mournful chime.

Art held his breath.

Inside, he could just make out the figures. Finch behind the counter, polishing something brass. The lad gestured to the box. Finch looked up, expression unreadable. There was a brief exchange. The lad's gestures became more animated, urgent even. Finch remained still, then shook his head, dismissive.

And then, something Art had never seen before.

Finch reached up and pulled the blinds.

Outside, the drizzle had turned heavier, muting the usual buzz of foot traffic. The market square, often bustling by mid-morning, was quieter than usual—no school groups, no deliveries, only the occasional umbrella bobbing past. Art squinted at the empty pavement and realised: If something had happened inside Finch's, it was entirely possible no one noticed. No witnesses. No eyes but his.

He kept the binoculars trained on the door. Five minutes. Ten. No movement. No rucksack. No green headphones. No lad. Not out the front door, not down the visible side street. Finch's might be a labyrinth on the inside, with a back alley for deliveries, but that gate was always chained, never used by customers.

He lowered the binoculars, unease tightening in his chest like a drawn string. Probably nothing. Maybe a private deal. But it was a break in routine—and Art lived by routine.

The rest of Monday passed in a blur of market noise and background TV. But the lad didn't reappear. No sign of him at all.

Tuesday morning brought more of the same. Mrs Henderson, right on cue. Gary, whistling like a dying kettle. Lamppost Larry, leg lifted in loyalty. But no rucksack. No lad.

At 11:00 a.m. sharp, a knock rattled the flat.

"Morning, Uncle Art!" Sarah's voice was always a little too cheerful for his taste. She bustled in with a bag of shopping, ponytail half-falling, dark circles beneath her eyes. "Milk, bread, that fancy biscuit you like. And the Telegraph."

"Already got it," Art muttered. "Milk's still cold too."

Sarah sighed. "What's got you twitching at the window today? More theories about alien pigeons?"

"It's the lad," he said.

She paused at the kettle. "What lad?"

"The one with the rucksack. Bright orange. Neon-green headphones—like glow sticks. Walks past Finch's Curios every morning. Gets his coffee from The Grind—like clockwork. He was there yesterday—went into Finch's. But he never came out. And today? Nothing."

Sarah raised an eyebrow. "You're still people-watching like it's some sort of street play?"

"It's observation," Art snapped. "And it's precise."

She gave a half-smile but moved to the window anyway, curiosity tugging at her. Down below, the town centre blurred with its usual weekday churn.

But if the lad had changed his routine, why go inside Finch's? Why stare at that box like it meant something? Art had seen obsession before—it always started small, then spiralled.

"He's probably got a cold. Or decided to take a different route. Maybe just fancied a lie-in for once."

Art shook his head. "No. He stopped. Looked at that new box in Finch's window. Then went in. Finch pulled the blinds. And he never came out."

Sarah turned slightly, her tone shifting—not alarmed, but thoughtful. "You do realise how that sounds?"

"I know what I saw."

It wasn't the first time he'd clocked someone in distress—he'd seen that look before, back when the mills were shutting down. People who were about to vanish from a life they'd built. And that lad, with his stop-and-stare urgency... he wasn't just shopping for antiques.

She stayed quiet for a beat. "Alright. I'll keep an eye out. Might ask at the coffee place tomorrow. No promises."

Art relaxed a little, just enough to blink. "Check the box too. It's new. Doesn't fit in. Could be something."

"I'll see what I can do," she said, heading into the kitchen. "But you're still buying me a brew if this turns out to be one of your wild goose chases."

He didn't answer. His gaze stayed fixed on Finch's Curios, as if waiting for something the rest of the world had missed.

Later that Tuesday, Sarah considered Art's words more than she cared to admit. She didn't have time to stop at The Grind that day, but she made a mental note to swing by in the morning. If anyone knew the lad's habits—the one with the bright rucksack and green headphones—it'd be the barista. She also passed by Finch's, giving the window a longer glance. The wooden box was still there, surrounded by more clutter than ever. The shop felt closed off, dim, like it didn't want to be seen.

That evening, she gave Art a quiet update. She still sounded sceptical—maybe even more so out loud—but beneath her calm, a small sliver of unease had taken root.

By Wednesday, the lad was still missing.

Thursday, the same.

Art rang Sarah. "Three days now. This isn't just a lie-in."

Maureen, his part-time carer with a habit of barging in like a storm front, bustled through the door—as she did most nights—to check his medication and make sure he'd eaten something decent. Her visits came with a familiar mix of sarcasm and soft-hearted nagging, but even she seemed unsettled tonight.

"The town's quiet," she muttered, peering through the window beside him. "Too quiet, maybe."

By Friday morning, Art no longer had doubts.
Four full days.
The lad with the rucksack had vanished.
Darwen's rhythm had faltered—one beat, missing.
And only Art seemed to hear the silence that followed.

He couldn't shake the feeling: something was wrong.
And no one else had seen it.

CHAPTER TWO

The Town's Whispers

Friday morning brought drizzle and routine. Buses hissed at the curb, shopkeepers rolled up rattling shutters, and Darwen breathed in its usual grey hush. But for Arthur Pickering, the world remained off-kilter.

Four days. That's how long it had been since the lad with the orange rucksack had vanished inside Finch's. No one else seemed to notice, but to Art, it was like a note missing from a song—subtle, but jarring.

Sarah was back, seated at the kitchen table with her hands wrapped around a steaming mug. She'd taken to checking in more regularly since Monday. Whether it was genuine concern or guilt over writing him off at first, Art couldn't tell.

"I still haven't seen him," Art said, watching the street from his window perch. "Not once since he went inside that shop."

Sarah nodded but didn't respond right away. She looked tired. Not just physically—mentally worn, like someone trying to keep their footing on uneven ground.

"I've asked around a bit," she said quietly. "The café staff remembered him. But the neighbours? The traders? No one's said a word. It's like he just vanished—and no one even noticed."

She shook her head. "It's not like this town. Usually, someone's always got something to say."

"I did pop into The Grind this morning," she said eventually. "You were right—they knew him. His name's Leo. Leo Davies."

She took a sip, then added, "Apparently, he came in almost every day. Flat white, headphones, history books. Bit of a regular. The barista—Chloe—said she hasn't seen him since Monday either."

Sarah hesitated. "She said she nearly reported it, actually. Chloe admitted she'd even called the non-emergency line, but they brushed her off. *'He's an adult, love,'* she mimicked. *'Give it a few more days. Happens all the time.'* She tried ringing him twice, but he didn't answer. And you know how it is—he's an adult, it's only been a few days. She figured maybe he'd just gone away for a bit. Still... she looked worried."

Art turned from the window. "So I'm not completely senile, then?"

"No," she said with a tired smile.

A pause settled between them. Sarah looked down into her mug, swirling the tea in slow, absent circles.

Art's voice was quiet. "Did she seem... close to him? Like they had a history?"

Sarah gave a small nod. "Yeah. I think there was a bit of a thing there. Nothing recent, but enough that she noticed when he stopped showing up."

She shifted in her seat. "I also asked if she knew where he lived. She mentioned the old mill flats by the foundry."

Art nodded slowly. "That tracks. He always came from that direction."

Another pause.

"I still think this could be nothing," Sarah said. "People vanish for a few days all the time. Maybe he just needed a break. Or maybe he left town."

"He didn't take anything with him," Art said, still staring through the binoculars. "No suitcase. No change in routine. People don't drop their patterns like that—not if nothing's wrong."

She sighed and didn't argue.

Maureen arrived just after midday, letting herself in with her usual firm knock and rustle of plastic bags. She greeted Art with a nod and set the carrier on the table.

"Your prescription," she said. "And some fresh bread. You looked like you were down on crusts yesterday."

"Crusts and conspiracy," Art muttered. "That's me lately."

Sarah rolled her eyes. "He's still on about the missing lad."

Maureen paused mid-unpacking. "Oh, that one? Rucksack boy? You said he went into Finch's and never came out?"

"Exactly," Art said.

Maureen made a sound between a laugh and a grunt. "Could be he left through the back. That shop's a rabbit warren. My mum used to say you could walk in and come out in another decade."

Sarah snorted. "I'm more worried Art might be right."

That silenced the room for a moment.

"I don't know," Maureen said eventually, sitting down and rubbing her knees. "Maybe something did happen. Or maybe you've both got too much time and imagination. If you're that worried, talk to the police."

"We can't go to them with this," Sarah said. "There's no proof anything's wrong."

Art looked from one to the other. "Then we find some."

Sarah shook her head. "You're talking like this is an episode of *Morse*. He's just a lad with a backpack. That doesn't mean anything awful has happened."

"I didn't say murder," Art replied. "But something's not right."

There was another beat of silence before Maureen broke it with a sigh. "I'll keep an eye on Finch's, then. In case something else weird happens."

Art smiled faintly. "That's all I ask."

Sarah stood and stretched. "I've got to head to the library this afternoon—I'll poke around, see if anyone there knows him. You never know."

"Be subtle," Art said. "No need to make a fuss."

"I'm always subtle," she said, pulling on her coat.

Maureen raised an eyebrow. "You're about as subtle as a brass band in a lift."

Sarah flipped her hood up. "Cheers for the vote of confidence."

The flat door closed behind her, leaving the two older figures in the now-familiar quiet.

"She's worried," Art said, almost to himself.

Maureen nodded. "Yeah. So am I."

Outside, Darwen's drizzle became steady rain, pattering against the glass like a clock slowly ticking out of time.

CHAPTER THREE

Into the Silence

Friday evening settled over Darwen like a wool blanket—thick, scratchy, and soaked through. The clouds above the moors were low and sullen, mirroring the heaviness that clung to Art Pickering's flat.

Sarah had returned from The Grind and the library not with drama, but with a strange, quiet weight. She sat across from her uncle now, arms folded, a line deepening between her brows.

"The librarian—Mrs. Ellison—she seemed genuinely concerned when I spoke to her. I got the sense Leo was there often, researching."

Art nodded slowly, absorbing the information like medicine.

"And Chloe?" he asked, though he already knew the answer.

Sarah nodded. "Still no sign. She tried calling again—straight to voicemail."

Art's reply came with a dry crackle. "People like that don't just vanish."

They sat in silence for a beat. The only sound was the ticking of the grandfather clock and the occasional creak of the building settling around them.

Maureen arrived just after six, as usual, letting herself in with a grunt and a bag full of ready meals. She glanced between the two of them.

"Same tension, different day?" she asked, unzipping her coat.

Sarah stood to help unpack. "We've confirmed his name—Leo Davies. Chloe said he lives at the Mill Apartments near the foundry. And he'd been spending a lot of time at the library lately. Digging into something."

Maureen paused. "Anything else?"

Sarah shook her head. "Not much. Just that he hasn't been in all week. She tried calling him—straight to voicemail."

Maureen didn't answer immediately. She made tea, her movements slow and deliberate.

"Look," she said eventually, setting down the mugs, "I still don't love this. We're making a lot of guesses. Maybe he had a breakdown. Maybe he's with family. Maybe he lost his phone and doesn't want to be found. But…"

She glanced at Art.

"But you've never been wrong about someone going missing before, have you?"

Art didn't gloat. He just looked tired.

"I've seen this town run like clockwork my whole life," he said. "And when a cog slips out—when someone like Leo disappears without a trace—it's not nothing."

The wind pressed against the window like a restless thought.

"I think," Sarah said carefully, "that we need to see if we can find where he lived. Just check the building. See if we can spot anything. A missed parcel. A knocked-over bin. Something."

Maureen raised an eyebrow. "We'd be pushing boundaries."

Sarah nodded. "Only a little. A knock on the door isn't a crime."

Art leaned forward. "You don't need to break the law. Just find a thread to pull."

Sarah finished her tea in one go. "I'll go in the morning."

Maureen sighed and pushed her mug away. "I'm coming with you. Two people look less suspicious."

Sarah smiled faintly. "I thought you'd say that."

They left it there. No great plan, no dramatic turning point. Just a quiet decision, shared between three people who had learned to read between the lines of routine.

Outside, Darwen's streets gleamed under the orange glow of streetlights. Somewhere, Leo Davies was either safe and silent... or missing and unheard.

Art didn't sleep well that night.

CHAPTER FOUR

Echoes in the Mill

Saturday morning came grey and quiet. A fine mist clung to the rooftops as Sarah and Maureen walked in silence, their footsteps soft on the damp pavements. Ahead of them, the Mill Apartments rose out of the old industrial quarter like a monument to contradiction—sleek glass framed by soot-stained brick, history swallowed by modernity.

Sarah tugged her coat tighter. "This still feels wrong."

Maureen shot her a glance. "So don't knock."

They stopped outside the communal entrance. The air smelled faintly of old metal and damp stone—a ghost of the Blackwood Foundry that once roared nearby.

Sarah sighed. "What if he's just on holiday? Or sleeping off a cold? And here we are, turning detective over someone who didn't ask to be noticed."

Maureen shrugged, calm as ever. "Then we apologise. But Leo's routine didn't just shift. It stopped. That's different."

They stepped into the lobby—a clean, modern space with pale walls and laminate flooring. The hum of fluorescent lighting filled the air.

Sarah scanned the digital directory. "3B. Leo Davies."

"Third floor," Maureen said, nodding towards the lift.

The ascent was slow and mechanical, the kind of silence that made their thoughts louder. Sarah checked her phone, knowing there'd be no new messages. At the top, they stepped out into a quiet corridor carpeted in muted grey. Every door looked the same —generic, anonymous.

They reached 3B.

Sarah hesitated, then knocked.

Nothing.

She waited five seconds and knocked again, harder this time. Still nothing.

She glanced at Maureen. "No footsteps. No sound. Not even a telly."

"Try again," Maureen said, but softly.

Sarah knocked once more, then pressed her ear against the wood. The door was cold. The silence on the other side felt deliberate, somehow.

"He's either not here," she murmured, "or he doesn't want to be found."

Maureen looked up and down the corridor. No movement. No neighbours. "I don't suppose he left a note saying, *'Gone into hiding. Back Monday'*?"

Sarah huffed a dry laugh, despite herself. "No such luck."

They stood in silence for a moment longer. Then Maureen leaned in, voice low. "If he left in a hurry, there might be signs. Something knocked over. Post piling up. I'll check his mailbox downstairs, see if I can spot anything in his windows from outside."

Sarah nodded. She crouched slightly, peering at the door edges, the floor. No scuffs. No signs of force. She tried the handle—locked, as expected.

Downstairs, Maureen circled the side of the building, scanning the rows of windows. After a few minutes, she returned, shaking her head.

"Curtains drawn. Nothing obvious. Mailbox has a few letters in."

Just as they turned to leave, the sound of a door creaking open echoed behind them. A man in joggers and a hoodie appeared in the corridor, holding a recycling bag. He eyed them warily.

Sarah offered a smile. "Sorry—we were just trying to get hold of Leo. 3B. We're a bit concerned."

The man hesitated. "Haven't seen him. Quiet bloke. Always with headphones on."

"Did you hear anything unusual this week?" Maureen asked.

He shook his head. "I keep to myself." And with that, he turned and disappeared down the stairs without another word.

"Friendly," Maureen muttered.

A second door opened slowly—this one revealing an elderly woman in a dressing gown and fluffy slippers, her grey hair in soft waves. Mrs. Albright, as she would soon introduce herself, looked them over with narrowed eyes before softening.

"You asking about the young lad?" she said. "Tall, orange rucksack?"

"Yes," Sarah said quickly. "Leo."

The woman stepped out further, voice lowering. "Monday night. There was a bit of fuss—I didn't see much, but I heard movement in the corridor. Around midnight. Then, not long after, a van— dark thing, no markings—backed right up to the side gate. Engine running for a bit."

Sarah's skin prickled. "Did you see anyone with him?"

"No. Just heard the door. And then it was quiet." Her flat faced the rarely used service entrance, and at that hour, the whole town usually went utterly silent. She'd heard it clearly—but who else would have?

Maureen stepped forward. "Did you tell anyone?"

The woman scoffed. "Who'd listen to me? Could've been a late-night taxi, for all anyone cares. Besides, they never believed me about the rattling pipes, let alone a van at midnight. But he hasn't been back since, has he?"

Sarah shook her head. "We don't think so."

"Well," the woman said, retreating into her flat, "you didn't hear it from me."

They waited until the door clicked shut behind her.

"I thought this would ease my mind," Sarah said.

"And now?" Maureen asked.

"I just feel more sure something's not right."

They left quietly. As the lift hummed back down, Sarah stared at the digital floor numbers.

"What now?"

"Talk to Art," Maureen said. "He'll want to know. And maybe it's time we dig into this Finch connection. Leo didn't just walk into that shop on a whim."

Outside, the mist had thickened. The brickwork of the mill cast long shadows across the street, stretching toward the foundry ruins like fingers reaching into the past.

The town was quiet. But something under its skin was beginning to stir.

Sarah stared down the road for a long moment before speaking. "If Leo was onto something, we need to figure out what. Maybe the library has a trail he left behind."

Maureen nodded, tucking her hands deeper into her pockets. "Old families, old money—it's always buried in paper."

They set off down the street, the mist thickening behind them.

CHAPTER FIVE

The Archivist's Echoes

The silence in Art's flat was heavy, broken only by the distant hum of the town and the gentle ticking of the grandfather clock. Sarah and Maureen sat opposite him, their faces grim. The weight of Mrs. Albright's account settled over them like a cold, damp fog. Movement in the corridor. A dark, unmarked van at midnight. It was no longer just a vague disappearance.

"He was taken," Art said, his voice flat and matter-of-fact. His binoculars lay forgotten on the windowsill, his gaze fixed on the middle distance, seeing not the street below but the chilling tableau Mrs. Albright had described. "Finch knew Leo was too close. He took him—and whatever he'd found."

Sarah shivered despite the warmth of the flat. "But why? What could Leo have found that was so important? And where would Finch take him?"

Maureen, ever the pragmatist, tapped a finger against her mug. "If Leo was 'digging into something,' like the librarian said, he probably carried it with him—his notes, his laptop— likely gone with him."

Art finally turned away from the window. His eyes, though tired, held a familiar flicker of intensity. "Leo was meticulous. You said he spent hours in the library, Sarah — the local history section. He must've used their digital archives. Maps, family records, old mill accounts. If he was chasing something, he might've left a breadcrumb trail behind."

Sarah nodded, the bones of a plan beginning to take shape. "The library. Mrs. Ellison already noticed he hasn't been in all week. She seemed concerned when I spoke to her—she might be willing to help."

"It's a long shot," Maureen said. "They can't just give you access to someone's data."

"No," Art agreed, "but they can show you what's public. What he looked at most. If he was pulling threads, they'll still be there."

The Darwen Library, normally a sanctuary of quiet focus, felt charged with something else that Saturday afternoon. The air— heavy with the scent of dust, paper, and polish — seemed to carry a quiet urgency.

Sarah found Mrs. Ellison at the local history desk, carefully cataloguing a box of faded photographs. She looked up, eyes immediately registering Sarah's return and the tension on her face.

"Any word?" she asked gently.

Sarah shook her head. "Not yet. But we think Leo's research might point to what he was onto. Or where he's gone."

She explained, gently, that Leo hadn't been seen since Monday and mentioned his routine—how he often passed Finch's Curios and spent hours in the library archives. She hinted that something about his research might be important, without going too far or speculating aloud.

Mrs. Ellison listened quietly, her expression slowly tightening with concern. "He said something to me the last time he was in," she murmured. "Something about shaking up what people thought they knew about Darwen. He was so passionate. And then he just… stopped coming."

She hesitated. "I can't share anything private, of course, but I can show you what he kept coming back to. The databases. The digital archives. He had patterns."

Sarah followed her to a quiet corner of the archives where a row of ageing computer terminals sat beneath narrow windows. Mrs. Ellison pointed to one near the end.

"He usually used that one. Hours at a time. Late some nights. He focused a lot on the Ainsworth family—old mill owners. Their papers are digitised. Business ledgers, personal letters, property deeds."

Sarah nodded, settling at the terminal.

Mrs. Ellison lowered her voice. "He looked into Blackwood Foundry quite a bit too. It came up alongside the Ainsworth records—old ledgers, land agreements. He seemed interested in how everything connected."

Then she quietly stepped back and left Sarah to work. Maureen headed off to get some coffees, realising they were in for the long haul.

Sarah opened the local archives database. She searched "Ainsworth family," "Blackwood Foundry," and "land records." Files unfolded across the screen—a labyrinth of scanned documents, grainy photos, and transcribed letters.

She worked for what felt like hours. Names blurred, dates ran together. The Ainsworths had investments in rail, coal, and several mills—including the Blackwood Foundry. There were ledgers, property maps, wills. But no clear trail.

Just as Sarah was about to give up, she noticed something odd in one of the Ainsworth ledger indexes—a brief reference to a subfolder titled simply *Anomalies*. It wasn't listed with the other family documents, almost like it had been mislabelled or added manually.

Her brow furrowed. "Maureen," she called quietly, waving her over. "Come and have a look at this."

She clicked.

Inside was a single file—not a document, but a compressed

archive. Its name looked strange: *doc_324alpha.zip.* She frowned. It didn't match the naming style of the other records.

She'd seen the number before—scattered throughout the Ainsworth documents. A photograph of a loom part stamped 'A324'. A letter dated 1897 referring cryptically to "Unit 3/2/4—decommissioned due to incident." She hadn't thought much of it until now.

Leo hadn't been leaving a trail. He was following one—one that someone tried to bury.

Sarah downloaded it and clicked to open—A password prompt appeared the moment she clicked.

Of course.

She stared at the blinking field, thinking hard. Leo had been careful. Mrs. Ellison said he'd write down odd phrases and numbers before searching. Sarah reached for the scrap of paper she'd been jotting on—terms and dates she'd scrawled down from her research. One number kept surfacing: 324. A street address? A date? A code?

She tried 324. Access denied.
0324. Nothing.
Three-two-four.
Ainsworth324. Still locked.

She leaned back, chewing her thumbnail, frustration mounting.

Then she remembered the cryptic reference in the 1897 letter: "Unit 3/2/4—decommissioned due to incident." The number 324, yes, but also that significant year. It wasn't just a number; it was a timestamp. Taking a breath, she typed 1897324. This time, the screen blinked. The archive opened.

Inside was a grainy image—a wooden box, ornately carved, unmistakable even in low resolution. The same one from Finch's Curios window.

Next to it, a file titled FOUND.txt.

They leaned in together, scrolling carefully through the entries. When they opened the subfolder, both women froze.

Beneath the Blackwood's heart, where the molten river sleeps,
A brass cylinder its secret keeps.
Three-two-four, the rhythm to unlock,
The first step on the path, before the final shock.

They stared at the screen, hearts thudding, amazed by what they were looking at.

Leo hadn't just stumbled on a connection. He'd gone out of his way to hide what he found—zipped behind a password, buried in a folder made to look like a forgotten mill ledger.

He was protecting something.
Or warning someone.

Sarah saved everything to her USB, fingers flying, then logged out in haste.

As they gathered their notes, Sarah paused.

"Mrs. Ellison said something earlier," she said, lowering her voice. "She told me she mentioned Leo's absence to the front desk—said it was odd he hadn't turned up all week."

"And?" Maureen asked, still scanning the last page.

"They said unless someone reports him officially—a parent or guardian—there's nothing they can do. He's an adult. People go missing for a few days all the time."

"Bloody ridiculous," Maureen muttered. "People vanish because everyone assumes someone else will care enough to report it."

Outside, the library was quieting. Evening crept in through the windows.

They stepped into the fading light, pulses still fluttering. The air was colder now, the streets quieter. Yet everything felt sharper— as if the town itself were holding its breath.

The first clue was in their possession.

And it pointed to Blackwood Foundry.

CHAPTER SIX

The Foundry's Echoes

Evening had settled over Darwen, the sky bruised purple and grey. Sarah and Maureen burst through Art's flat, breathless, a small USB clutched in Sarah's hand like a talisman. Maureen perched herself on the edge of Art's armchair, her gaze fixed on the still-closed blinds of Finch's Curios. Tension filled the flat—five days of Leo's silence pressing on them like fog.

"We found it," Sarah gasped, her voice tight with a mix of exhaustion and exhilaration. She fumbled with the laptop, plugging in the USB. "At the library. His research. He was onto something. Something significant."

Art leaned forward, his eyes fixed on the glowing screen as Sarah navigated to "*doc_324alpha.zip*" folder. She displayed the blurred image of the wooden box, then the cryptic text document.

Art's gnarled finger traced the words on the screen.
"Beneath the Blackwood's heart, where the molten river sleeps,
A brass cylinder its secret keeps.
Three-two-four, the rhythm to unlock,
The first step on the path, before the final shock."

"The Blackwood Foundry," Art murmured, his eyes alight with a familiar, almost youthful intensity. "I knew it. He was digging into the Ainsworths' industrial connections. The Blackwood was one of the largest foundries in the area, supplied many of the mills. And the Ainsworths had a significant stake in it." He paused, frowning in thought. "The 'molten river' must be the casting floor—where molten metal once flowed like lava, forging the very components that powered Darwen's textile industry."

"And a brass cylinder," Maureen added. "Hidden there. Leo must have found this riddle—or the cylinder itself—before he went to Finch's. That's why he went there."

"And Finch took him," Sarah finished, the words chilling in the quiet room. "He took Leo, and his rucksack, and presumably any other research Leo had on him. He knew Leo was too close."

She looked again at the riddle. "Three-two-four, the rhythm to unlock. What does that mean? A combination? A sequence? A code?"

Art sat back for a moment, then reached behind him and pulled a thick, battered book from a pile on the sideboard. He let it thud onto the coffee table between them and flipped to a dog-eared section.

"Blackwood Foundry," he said. "Blueprints. This was from a failed preservation project back in the nineties. I always kept it—just in case."

The diagrams were detailed and dense, but Art navigated them with ease. "Here. This was the main casting floor—see the channel layout? That's where molten metal flowed. The central furnace sat here. And right next to it, this square—possibly an old maintenance shaft or waste access. If Leo's clue is right, this could be the 'heart' of the foundry."

Sarah leaned over, tracing the map. "So we'd enter here, past the collapsed loading bay, then cut through this side corridor…"

"Stick to the perimeter," Art advised. "That roof's likely collapsed by now. Look for the chimney base—that's your anchor point. Once you find that, you'll be close."

Maureen closed the book, nodding. "Better than stumbling in blind."

As the three of them sat in silence, the weight of the situation settled heavily around them. Each wondered if they were crossing a line they couldn't step back from.

Art met their eyes. "It's dangerous. Finch may already know Leo went there. If he's watching, be careful. But you need to go. You need to know what Leo found."

The Blackwood Foundry loomed against the bruised evening sky, a skeletal silhouette of rusted iron and crumbling brick. Its immense, cavernous structure, once a roaring heart of industry, now stood silent—a decaying monument to a forgotten era.

The air was heavy with the scent of damp concrete and metallic decay.

They approached cautiously, footsteps muffled by weeds and broken tarmac. Sarah held Art's military-grade torch, its beam slicing the gloom. Maureen walked beside her, a small utility knife hidden in her coat pocket, eyes sharp for movement. Every creak of metal, every shift of shadow, made them pause.

The rusted iron fence surrounding the site had partially collapsed near the rear. They squeezed through, emerging into the vast courtyard beyond.

Inside, the foundry felt like another world. Towering brick walls stretched overhead, some stripped of their roofs. Twisted girders and shattered windows loomed like jagged teeth. Pools of stagnant water reflected the torchlight in warped, shivering shapes.

Sarah's voice echoed faintly. "The Blackwood's heart. The molten river."

Guided by Art's directions, they moved deeper into the foundry's centre. Their boots crunched over broken glass and soot-blackened tiles. Dust hung thick in the air, disturbed only by their cautious breath.

They found it—a wide-open space dominated by the remains of the main furnace. The channels carved into the concrete floor suggested where molten metal once flowed like lava. And just to the left, near a collapsed wall, something out of place: a manhole cover, rusted but clearly disturbed.

Sarah crouched, brushing away debris. Fresh scrape marks scored the concrete — recent, undeniable.

"This was moved," she whispered.

Using a length of rebar, they pried it open. The cold breath of the shaft rushed up to meet them—damp, earthy, stale. A narrow chamber lay below, brick-lined and dark.

"I'll go," Sarah said firmly. "You keep watch."

Carefully, she lowered herself into the shaft, torch clenched between her teeth. The walls were slick. The air close and musty.

She landed with a splash. The space was tight — barely enough to stand. Her light swept the room—rubble, broken piping, water damage.

Then, tucked beneath a collapsed pipe, a recess in the wall—and in it, only disturbed brick and tool marks.

"It's gone," Sarah whispered. "It was here. But someone's already taken it."

Maureen knelt above. "Finch."

Sarah nodded, heart pounding. "Leo must've found the cylinder. And when he vanished... so did it."

Maureen's jaw tightened. "Then Finch must have taken it from Leo. He took Leo. And took this."

Sarah's mind raced. "But he doesn't have the riddle. He won't know how to open it."

From somewhere deeper in the foundry came the scrape of movement. A scuttle. Fast. Too fast for a person. Rat? Fox?

They froze.

Then silence.

They didn't wait to find out.

As Sarah climbed from the shaft, the meaning of Leo's clue pressed in on her like the weight of the sky: the cylinder had been real, and it had been stolen.

But the knowledge—the sequence—that was still theirs.

And if they were right... this was only the beginning.

CHAPTER SEVEN

A Moth in the Curio Shop

The sharp snap in the Blackwood Foundry had sent a jolt of pure terror through Sarah and Maureen, freezing them in the damp, echoing chamber. Sarah, having clambered out of the shaft, now stood beside Maureen, both of them rigid by the opened manhole cover, breath held. The silence that followed was suffocating, broken only by the frantic thumping of their own hearts.

Then, a faint, almost apologetic whine. A rustle of dry leaves — and a small, scruffy terrier trotted into the edge of Sarah's torchlight, tail wagging tentatively. It sniffed at a pile of rubble, then lifted its leg against a rusted girder, utterly oblivious to the drama it had just caused. A moment later, a gruff voice called out, "Come on, boy! Let's go!" A distant figure, silhouetted in the entrance, appeared with a leash in hand.

Sarah let out a long, shuddering breath — a mix of relief and fading adrenaline. Maureen sagged against the heavy iron manhole cover.

"Just… just a dog," Maureen whispered, a shaky laugh escaping her lips.

They quickly replaced the heavy cover with a combined effort, pushing the disturbed earth back around its edges. The immediate threat had been a false alarm, but the chilling discovery remained: Leo had been here. He had found the brass cylinder. And then Finch had taken him — and the cylinder.

Back in Art's flat, the small USB stick now plugged into his laptop, the blurred image of the wooden box and the cryptic riddle glowed on the screen. The air was thick with the scent of Art's strong tea — a comforting anchor amid the grim realisation.

"So, he found it," Art said, his voice unusually flat, an edge of cold analysis creeping in. He traced the words on the screen:

"Beneath the Blackwood's heart, where the molten river sleeps,
A brass cylinder its secret keeps.
Three-two-four, the rhythm to unlock,
The first step on the path, before the final shock."

"He found the cylinder at the foundry," Sarah confirmed, her voice rough with cold and fear. "But it was gone. Finch must have taken it from him. Along with his rucksack. And anything else Leo had on him."

"And the three-two-four sequence," Maureen added, her tone quiet but sure. "Finch has the cylinder, but he doesn't know how to open it. That clue — it was buried in the archives. Leo found it. But it wasn't his clue to begin with. It's been hidden a long time."

The realisation hung heavy between them. It was their only advantage in what now felt like a far more dangerous game. Finch had the object — but not the knowledge. And Leo was still missing.

"We need to get into Finch's Curios," Sarah said quietly. "We need to get that cylinder. And we need to find out where Leo is."

Art nodded slowly, his eyes narrowing as he looked across the street toward the antique shop. "It won't be easy. Finch is cautious. And now, he'll be on edge. He knows Leo was close. He'll be guarding whatever he took."

"We can't break in," Maureen said. "And we've got nothing solid to go to the police with. The last thing they'll listen to is a hunch and a riddle."

"No," Art agreed. "But we can make our own way in. Finch is meticulous, but he's also proud. He thinks of himself as a curator, not a shopkeeper. You'll need a reason to be there — a proper one.

Something that'll get him talking. Distracted."

Maureen folded her arms. "So, we go in as what? Browsers?"

"Collectors," Art replied. "Sarah, you can be curious. Enthusiastic. Ask about something specific. Something rare, obscure. He'll take the bait. Finch likes to show off. He might even disappear into the back. And while he's distracted…"

Maureen's expression shifted as the idea clicked. "I look."

Art nodded. "Quickly. You don't open anything unless it's already ajar. No drawers. No forcing locks. If there's anything hidden, it'll be close to hand. Finch doesn't take risks — he'll keep the important stuff within reach."

"What kind of item would distract him?" Sarah asked.

Art looked around his cluttered bookshelf and pointed to a worn volume of *Darwen's Forgotten Trades*. "Mill parts. Anything brass. Ask about Darwen loom shuttles or precision-made components. That'll appeal to his pride. You don't even have to know what you're talking about — he'll do the talking for you."

It was dangerous. But it was the only plan they had.

Sunday passed in uneasy silence. Sarah and Maureen stayed close to Art's flat, watching Finch's shop from behind twitching curtains. Finch didn't open. But at some point during the afternoon, the wooden box vanished from the display. One moment it was there — the next, gone. They didn't risk a move. Not yet…

Monday morning was clear and sharp with cold. The town centre buzzed with life — children tugging parents toward bakeries, market stalls calling out deals — the ordinary world moving on, indifferent to the darker current beneath its surface.

Across the road from Finch's Curios, Sarah and Maureen watched the man himself wipe down his window. Same as ever. The wooden box, gone since yesterday, hadn't returned to the display.

"Ready?" Maureen asked.

Sarah nodded. "Let's make this quick."

The bell above the door gave a dry, metallic chime as they stepped inside. The shop was as they remembered — dim, dusty, and stuffed to the rafters with things that once mattered to someone. Furniture towered in corners. Shelves heaved with relics and obscurities. The scent of old varnish and paper filled the air.

Mr. Finch appeared from behind the counter like a figure summoned from the gloom. "Ladies," he said, polite but wary. "How can I assist?"

"We heard you had some interesting local pieces," Sarah said with an easy smile. "Industrial relics. My uncle mentioned something about an early Darwen loom shuttle with brass fittings."

Finch blinked — the flicker of interest there, just as Art predicted. "I may have such a thing. Not on display, of course. The finer pieces are kept in my secure collection."

"Oh, of course," Sarah replied, clasping her hands innocently. "We're quite fascinated by Darwen's industrial history. Especially rare items."

Finch gave a small bow of the head. "Then allow me a moment."

He slipped behind a velvet curtain toward the back.

Maureen moved. Smooth, practiced. She scanned the room, her eyes pausing on the counter. Below it, barely visible, was a polished wooden chest — far newer than anything else in sight. On its lid: a small engraving. A falcon, wings tucked.

The wooden box.

She reached out and brushed a finger across it — not enough to shift it, just enough to mark it in her mind. It was locked. But it was there.

Finch's footsteps were already returning.

Maureen turned away just in time, blending into the shadows

between two leaning bookcases as Sarah continued her careful performance — asking about textile mills, marvelling at a dusty set of callipers, giving Finch just enough reason to keep talking.

They hadn't found Leo. Not yet.

But they'd found where the secrets were hiding.

And now, they had to find a way to unlock them — before Finch realised they were getting too close.

CHAPTER EIGHT

The Falcon's Riddle

The heavy velvet curtain swayed, then settled, muffling the sound of Finch's retreating footsteps. Maureen's heart hammered against her ribs — a frantic drumbeat in the sudden, dust-laden silence of the shop. This was it. Her window of opportunity. She knew it wouldn't last long.

Her eyes darted to the small, ornate wooden box tucked beneath the counter. It was the same box Art had seen in the window on Monday — the one from Leo's blurred library photo. Its polished rosewood gleamed faintly, and on its lid, the distinctive silver inlay of a peregrine falcon seemed to watch her, unblinking. It was beautiful, unsettling — and almost certainly the key to Leo's final discovery.

Maureen's fingers brushed the surface. It wasn't locked — just secured by a small, discreet clasp near the lid. Her thumb flicked it open with a soft click.

She hesitated, listening for Finch's footsteps beyond the curtain. Then, carefully, she lifted the lid.

Inside, nestled against a velvet lining, lay the brass cylinder. Just as Leo's riddle had described — about the size of a large cigar, tarnished, but unmistakably brass. Maureen snatched it, her fingers closing around its cool, smooth surface. It was sealed tight, no obvious opening — but that didn't matter now. Her priority was to get out.

She tucked the brass cylinder deep into her coat pocket, then gently closed the box, ensuring the lid clicked back into place, and slid it back beneath the counter. Everything looked exactly as it had before.

Maureen moved through the shop, feigning interest in dusty shelves, eyes darting nervously for any sign of Leo's rucksack or his notes — anything that might hint at his whereabouts. Nothing. The space was crammed with antique clutter, but no orange-and-blue rucksack. No discarded papers. Finch had been thorough.

Footsteps. Closer now. Finch was returning.

"Anything?" Sarah's voice called out from the front of the shop — slightly too loud, a little too animated. Still holding his attention.

Maureen finished her scan and drifted back toward the front just as the velvet curtain rustled. Finch emerged, a dusty loom shuttle in hand, a thin, triumphant smile on his face.

"A rare piece, indeed, madam. From the earliest Darwen mills. Pre-dates the great fire of 1850," he said, holding it out.

Sarah, catching Maureen's eye, forced a look of fascination. "Remarkable! The craftsmanship is exquisite. My uncle will be thrilled." She took the shuttle, turning it in her hands, buying precious seconds.

"We'll take it," Sarah said, glancing at Maureen, who gave a barely perceptible nod. "How much do we owe you, Mr. Finch?"

Finch's smile widened, a glint of greed in his eyes. He launched into a long-winded explanation of the item's provenance. Sarah quickly completed the transaction.

"Thank you for your time, Mr. Finch," she said, clutching the shuttle. "We must be going."

"Indeed," Finch replied, his gaze lingering a moment too long. "Do come again."

The door's bell gave a mournful chime as they stepped outside.

The Darwen sunlight, once comforting, now felt stark and exposing.

A block away, they stopped, their breaths ragged — relief at the escape tempered by the weight of what they'd found.

"Did you get it?" Sarah asked, breathless.

Maureen pulled the brass cylinder from her pocket. "Yes. This is it."

Sarah glanced back at the shop. "If Leo was ever in there, he's not now."

Maureen nodded grimly. "Too much junk. Not many places to hide something — or someone."

Sarah's voice dropped. "What if he moved him? Waited until the shops were shut. Took him out the back — through the ginnel or a side door. No one would've seen a thing."

Maureen's expression darkened. "Then we're already days too late."

She turned the cylinder in her hand. "But why the hell would he still have it?"

"And Leo..." Sarah murmured, "He probably didn't think it was dangerous. Chloe said he was private, but obsessed — always scribbling notes, following threads no one else noticed. He might've thought it was just an old mystery. Something academic."

Maureen exhaled slowly. "Didn't realise what he'd stumbled into."

Sarah nodded. "Not until it was too late."

They hurried back to Art's flat. The Darwen afternoon now felt colder, the shadows longer. Maureen placed the brass cylinder on the coffee table beside the loom shuttle.

Art's gnarled finger traced the familiar riddle on the laptop screen:

"Beneath the Blackwood's heart, where the molten river sleeps,
A brass cylinder its secret keeps.

Three-two-four, the rhythm to unlock,
The first step on the path, before the final shock."

"This is it," Art murmured, eyes locked on the cylinder. "The rhythm to unlock. Three-two-four."

Sarah examined it under the laptop's glow. Faint, almost invisible lines were etched into its surface, dividing it into sections — and near one end, a tiny arrow.

"It's a twist," Sarah said. "Look — the lines. The arrow. It's a sequence of turns."

She held the cylinder firmly. She twisted the top section three times clockwise. A faint click. Then the middle section, twice counter-clockwise. Another click. Finally, four turns clockwise on the bottom section.

With a soft, ethereal hiss, the top of the cylinder sprang open.

Inside, nestled in faded velvet, was a tightly rolled parchment, yellowed and brittle. It was bound with a thread so fine it was nearly invisible.

Sarah retrieved it carefully. As she unrolled it, an image shimmered into view — a stylised drawing of Darwen Tower.

Beside it, elegant faded script, interspersed with a precise, almost scientific diagram:

"Where Darwen's gaze meets the sky, a silent witness stands,
The beacon's heart, within the highest lands.
Seek the compass rose, where winds converge,
A feather's touch, will secrets surge.
Three-two-four, the rhythm to reveal,
The final truth, the wounds to heal."

Sarah and Maureen stared at the parchment — then at each other. Another riddle. Another step. And the drawing — the box's first real secret.

Art's eyes lit up. "The Tower! Of course. 'Where Darwen's gaze meets the sky.' It watches the whole town. And 'the beacon's heart'

— the fire they lit on special occasions. A symbol of pride."

"And 'Seek the compass rose'," Maureen added. "There's a compass carved into the Tower's base. I remember it from years ago."

"And 'A feather's touch'," Sarah murmured. "What does that mean?"

Art leaned back, thoughtful. "The Ainsworth family crest. A peregrine falcon. Falcons shed feathers… maybe symbolic. Maybe a tool. Leo would've picked up on that."

"And again with 'three-two-four'," Maureen said. "It was the key to the cylinder. And now to this — the final truth."

The relief of escaping Finch's shop faded fast. A new mystery had taken its place.

The sun dipped lower, casting long shadows. Darwen Tower — distant, looming — beckoned from the moor.

The hunt wasn't over.

It had just moved to higher ground.

CHAPTER NINE

The Collector's Fury

Elias Finch emerged from the velvet curtain at the back of his shop, a faint smile playing on his thin lips. The loom shuttle — a genuine pre-Victorian piece — was gone now, sold off without a second thought. The two women — the niece and her aunt — had been surprisingly easy marks.

So keen on their local industrial history. He'd spun them a tale about the shuttle's provenance, added a few extra pounds to the price, and they'd swallowed it whole. Amateurs. They were always the easiest to fleece.

The chime of the bell still lingered in the dusty silence of the shop — a pleasant, musical note that signified profit. He liked the quiet after a sale: the scent of old varnish, the hush of the shop, the satisfying rustle of banknotes. He smoothed the crisp twenty-pound notes between gloved fingers and added them to the neat stack in the till. A good morning's work.

His gaze drifted to the small, ornate wooden box tucked discreetly beneath the counter. A valuable piece from his personal collection — acquired years ago, perhaps even from the Darwen Museum theft, though he'd never admit it aloud. It was beautiful, unsettling. And now, it held something even more precious.

Leo Davies had brought the brass cylinder to the shop on Monday, after unearthing it from the depths of the old Blackwood Foundry. Finch, realising Leo was too close to the truth, had acted quickly. The cylinder — along with Leo's rucksack and notes — was now his.

He'd placed the cylinder inside the wooden box for safekeeping. It was symbolic, almost poetic — a secret hidden in plain sight, tucked behind polished wood and velvet lining. The falcon emblem was a subtle nod to the Ainsworth legacy — a legacy he believed should be his, passed down through a lineage the world had conveniently forgotten.

Finch ran a gloved hand over the rosewood lid, admiring the craftsmanship, the gleam of the inlay. He had tried to open the cylinder, of course. Pressed, twisted, examined it under every light he owned. But the mechanism refused to yield. Forcing it risked damage — and he was a collector, not a butcher. The clues inside could be fragile. They might dissolve if exposed to the wrong conditions. He'd been patient so far. He could be patient a little longer.

Still, he'd decided it was time to move the box to the secure vault in the back. It was too valuable to leave even partially exposed. He reached for it, fingers closing around the familiar wood.

It felt lighter than it should.

A prickle of unease crept across his scalp. Brow furrowed, he set the box on the counter and flipped the lid.

The dark velvet lining was untouched. The recess, perfectly cut to cradle the cylinder, lay undisturbed.

But it was empty.

Finch stared, his mind stalling against the shock. No. No — it had to be here. He reached in, fingers scrabbling at the velvet, willing the object to reappear. Nothing. Just the void. The recess gaped like a wound.

The brass cylinder — gone.

Disbelief gave way to rising, acidic panic. He stood frozen for a beat. Then he snapped into motion. Spun on his heel. Scanned the counter. The shelves. Tore open drawers. Yanked aside cloths.

Upended stacks of books, sent them crashing to the floor. Nothing. Nothing.

The women.

He replayed their visit in his mind — Sarah's eager, wide-eyed questions. Her uncle's supposed obsession with loom shuttles. Maureen, quiet and observant, drifting through the shop. Too quiet. Too deliberate.

He remembered the way Sarah had watched him vanish behind the curtain. The way Maureen lingered near the counter. That nod exchanged just before they left.

Not curiosity. Collusion.

He'd been outsmarted.

By two women.

His fists clenched. The brass cylinder — *his* brass cylinder — was gone. The one he had taken from Leo. The one Leo had risked everything to find. And they'd walked in and stolen it from under his nose.

Rage flooded him, hot and sharp. He swept a shelf of tarnished silver to the floor. The crash rang through the shop. A stack of antique books followed. He overturned a chair. Dust rose like smoke.

He stormed to the front window and stared at the empty street. They were gone. But not far. They had help. Someone who had Leo's research. Someone who knew where to look.

Someone who thought this was a race.

Finch's breath came in sharp bursts. They didn't understand. They thought the cylinder *was* the treasure — but it was only the beginning. The first step. The opening thread in a much larger tapestry.

He still had Leo.

The boy was stubborn, but time wore down even the sharpest

minds. Finch would get what he needed from him.

And now, he had another reason to hurry.

He would find those women. He would take back what was his. And when he did, there would be no more polite smiles. No more salesmanship. No more velvet curtains.

The game had changed.

And Elias Finch was done playing fair.

CHAPTER TEN

The Beacon's Secret

The taxi dropped them at the edge of the moor, the last vestiges of daylight clinging stubbornly to the western horizon. A sharp wind whipped around them the moment they stepped out, tugging at their coats and hair with icy fingers. Darwen Tower loomed ahead — a stark, imposing silhouette etched against the bruised sky. Its beacon, though long extinguished, still stood as a silent promise.

The path up the moor was steep and uneven, treacherous in the fading light.

"It's a long way up," Maureen said, pulling her scarf tighter.

The silence of the moor was vast, broken only by the mournful cry of a distant curlew and the restless rustle of dry heather. Every shadow seemed to stretch unnaturally. Every rock took on an ominous shape.

They walked in silence, their breath rising in silver clouds. Sarah held Art's powerful torch, its beam cutting a narrow, dancing swathe through the gloom. They kept glancing over their shoulders — haunted by the image of Finch's furious face, by the memory of Mrs. Albright's sighting of the dark van. The isolation of the moor offered concealment… but amplified their vulnerability.

Finally, the Tower loomed directly above them — a colossal stone sentinel. Its sheer scale was breathtaking, its weathered walls a monument to centuries of Darwen's grit and history.

They circled to the wide, circular base, and there, etched into the rough-hewn stone, was the magnificent compass rose. Its cardinal points — N, S, E, W — and intercardinal marks stood weathered but clear.

Sarah swept the torchlight over the carving. The riddle echoed in her mind:
"Seek the compass rose, where winds converge,
A feather's touch, will secrets surge."

"A feather's touch," Maureen murmured, kneeling beside her. "Art said the Ainsworth crest was a peregrine falcon. Could there be a feather carved somewhere?"

They searched the compass rose meticulously, fingertips trailing over the cold stone, probing every groove and imperfection. The wind howled around the Tower, and the shadows played tricks with their vision.

Then — a glint. Sarah's torch beam caught something near the northwest edge of the rose. She crouched, brushing away grit and moss. There — nearly invisible — was a tiny carved feather, no larger than a thumbnail.

"Here," she whispered, tight with excitement. "The feather."

Maureen leaned in. "That's what the riddle meant — 'the feather's touch.'"

Just beneath it, Sarah felt a shallow dip — worn smooth, sunken slightly below the rest of the carving.

"This has been used before," Maureen murmured. "Worn down. Maybe walked over for years."

Sarah continued sweeping the outer edge with the torch. Small bronze inlays marked intervals along the ring — seemingly decorative. But some looked older. Duller. Subtly different.

"Three-two-four," she said softly. "It's a sequence."

She pressed the feather gently.

Then, turning clockwise, she counted three markers. A brass disc

— slightly recessed. She pressed it.

Click.

Back two markers counter-clockwise. A small carved triangle, faintly loose. She pressed again.

Click.

Then forward four more. A square brass stud, dulled with age.

Click.

For a moment, nothing.

Then, deep within the tower, came the slow grind of unseen cogs — the groan of metal stirred from sleep. Somewhere above, something shifted.

A narrow stone slit creaked open high in the beacon chamber. Behind it, a dust-covered lens assembly — long dormant - pivoted into place on an ancient brass rail. It caught the last slant of evening sun, low on the horizon.

As the light pierced through, it refracted in a tight, brilliant beam that swept across the moor.

It paused.

Then, with a final jolt, locked onto a precise point across the valley - the face of Darwen Town Hall's grand clock.

They stood frozen.

Sarah stared in awe. "The mechanism still works... after all this time. Someone built this to mark something. A day, a season. A direction."

The beam held, unwavering — a golden finger of light pointing from the old tower's heart to the clock face far below.

They exchanged a look — awe colliding with something darker. Because now they had found it.

Not an object.

A direction.

A bearing.

And suddenly, the line from the parchment - *"the turn of the heart will speak"* — took on a new, chilling meaning.
The Town Hall clock. Its heart. Its mechanism. That was the next step.

Sarah tore her gaze from the beam. "We can't leave it like this."

Maureen nodded, already moving. "Let's shut it down. No need to leave a beacon lit." Together, they retraced their steps to the control plate. With a reluctant creak, the lens assembly disengaged.
The beam faltered.
Then vanished.
Stone ground against stone as the slit slowly closed, swallowing the last of the light.

Silence returned to the tower.

As they turned to leave, a violent gust tore across the moor — howling like a warning. Dust and grit stung their faces. The Tower groaned, its stones shifting in protest. It was just the wind... just the moor. That's what they told themselves.

But the feeling of being watched lingered.

—

Back in the town centre, Elias Finch stood in the middle of his dimly lit shop.

The velvet-lined recess inside the music box lay empty — a gaping wound in his carefully guarded world.

He had checked again and again. The brass cylinder was gone.

His earlier rage had cooled. In its place: a cold, deliberate fury.

He knew who had taken it. Sarah and Maureen. Leo Davies's rescuers — or accomplices.

He had spent the afternoon examining the box. Every edge. Every groove. Tried every combination, every pressure point. Even brought out his finest tools.

Nothing.

They had opened it. And he hadn't.

Now they knew more than he did.

Through the window, he looked across the market street toward the row of flats.

Art Pickering's third-floor light was on.

And through the glass, silhouetted in lamplight, Finch could just make out two figures — heads bowed over something on a table. Something small. Cylindrical.

A grim, mirthless smile tugged at his lips.

They were celebrating. Right there. In plain view.

He had underestimated them.

But now? Now he knew exactly where they were.

And what they had.

The game had changed.

Finch still had Leo.

And he would use him to get back what was rightfully his.

CHAPTER ELEVEN

The Clockwork Heart

By the time Sarah and Maureen stumbled back into Art's flat, the Darwen evening had surrendered to a chill, starless night. Their breath came in ragged gasps—not just from the descent down the moor, but from the sheer, impossible spectacle they'd just witnessed. The ethereal beam of blue light, a silent, shimmering arrow from Darwen Tower to the Town Hall clock face, was burned into their retinas. It was a marvel—an ancient secret revealed in stone—and it filled them with awe, tinged with the terrifying realisation of what they were truly up against.

Art, still seated in his armchair by the window, looked up the moment they entered. His sharp eyes instantly picked up on their shaken state.

"Well?" he asked, voice low—laced with concern and urgency. "Did you find it? What did the Tower tell you?"

Sarah, still breathless, pulled the rolled parchment from her pocket. The edges were crumpled from their journey, but the drawing remained clear. She laid it flat on the coffee table, smoothing it with care.

"It pointed, Art," she whispered, voice still caught in wonder. "A beam of light. From the Tower straight to the Town Hall clock."

Maureen nodded. "It was... unbelievable. Like something out of a film. And the riddle—it fits. 'Where Darwen's gaze meets the sky'—that's the Tower. And the light, it pointed to the 'beacon's heart'—the Town Hall clock."

Art leaned in, tapping a gnarled finger on the parchment. He read the final lines aloud:
"Three-two-four, the rhythm to reveal,
The final truth, the wounds to heal."

He sat back, eyes narrowed in thought. "So, the same sequence. But applied to the clock. And 'the turn of the heart will speak'… it has to mean the mechanism itself. The inner workings."

The awe quickly gave way to strategy. They had the location. Now came the harder part—figuring out how the 'three-two-four' rhythm related to a century-old clock, and how to get inside the building without drawing attention.

"The Town Hall," Sarah said, pacing. "It's a public building, sure. But the clock tower? That'll be locked up. We can't break in—we're already pushing our luck."

Art was already flipping through a stack of Darwen history books beside his chair. "Built in the 1880s," he muttered. "Symbol of civic pride, cotton boom era. The domed tower originally held a weather vane… the clock came later, 1899. Potts of Leeds mechanism. Funded by Mayor Dr. James Ballantyne. Very precise. Hour-striking, weight-driven."

He pulled a thick, leather-bound volume into his lap, turning its fragile pages. "We need plans. Structural notes. Anything…"

Art's flat transformed into a makeshift command post. Books opened, maps unfurled, the laptop casting a steady glow as they pored through online archives. Art, with his encyclopaedic knowledge of Darwen, guided them through obscure facts and forgotten footnotes.

"The main entrance is out," he said, tracing a faded blueprint with his finger. "Too visible. But there was a service entrance. North side. Used to be for coal deliveries and maintenance. It leads to the boiler room, and probably hasn't seen much traffic in decades. That's your best bet."

"And the clock?" Maureen asked, studying a Victorian diagram of the mechanism. "How does 'three-two-four' work here? It's not a code we can just punch in."

Art tapped the diagram. "The 'heart' of a clock is the escapement—the part that controls the ticks. But I think it's more literal. The winding mechanism, maybe. Or the gearing." He pulled out a yellowed newspaper clipping. "Look—1903. An apprentice clockmaker got locked in the tower during a storm. Said he could 'make the clock sing' by touching specific cogs. Called it the 'song of the gears' and 'the rhythm of the pendulum.'"

Sarah's eyes widened. "That's it. A sequence. Touching certain gears, like the compass rose. A rhythm."

"Exactly," Art said. "Three touches, then two, then four. Or maybe it's a sequence of winding movements. Either way, it's meant to be subtle. You'd have to know what you were looking for."

They began planning.

They'd go during the day, blending in with visitors or staff. Maureen—calm, capable—would lead the approach. Sarah would play support, ready to talk, distract, adapt.

"We need a reason to be there," Sarah said. "Something that gets us into the tower itself."

"A research project," Art offered. "You're documenting Darwen's industrial heritage. The clock is an engineering marvel, and you've requested access to examine it."

Maureen nodded. "I'll pose as a university contact. Do a proper letter if needed. I'll dress the part. Sensible. Invisible."

Tension lingered beneath the surface. Finch. He'd seen them. He knew they had the cylinder. The thought crawled behind every word, every movement. Sarah's shoulders remained tight, her eyes flicking often to the window. Maureen checked the lock on the door twice.

"He'll be watching," Maureen murmured.

Art's expression darkened. "He will. Which is why you must be careful. Disappear into the crowd. No lingering. Get in, do what you must, and get out."

He looked at them—serious, eyes full of quiet desperation. "Leo is counting on you. And so am I."

They packed light—Art's torch, a notebook, a couple of pens. They'd go first thing in the morning, aiming for the busiest part of the day to disappear into the tide of activity.

The final truth lay hidden in the turning heart of Darwen's clock.

And Finch was out there, waiting.

CHAPTER TWELVE

The Final Turn

The morning sun, pale but determined, filtered through the grimy windows of Art's flat as Sarah and Maureen prepared. The air thrummed with nervous energy, a stark contrast to the quiet, scholarly calm of the previous night's research. Darwen Town Hall — a grand Victorian sentinel — awaited them, its clock tower now a beacon of both hope and danger.

"Remember the plan," Art said, his voice firm as his gaze swept over them. "Blend in. Look like you belong. Once you're in that clock tower, be quick. Finch might not know where you're heading — but he'll be watching."

Sarah, tightening her grip on the worn notebook, gave a small nod. "We'll keep our heads down. Take only what we need."

Maureen gave a quiet grunt of agreement as she checked the folded letter in her coat pocket.

Sarah, in a smart, unassuming coat, nodded, clutching a worn leather notebook. Maureen, dressed in sensible nurse's shoes and a plain cardigan, adjusted her glasses. They looked like ordinary citizens — perhaps local historians or postgraduate researchers. Their very ordinariness was their shield.

"We know, Art," Sarah said, trying to project confidence she didn't fully feel. "We'll be careful. And we'll find Leo."

The walk to the Town Hall blurred into a mix of nerves and anticipation. The market street buzzed with voices and footsteps, helping them disappear into the crowd. The Town Hall loomed ahead — proud and stone-faced, its tower rising against the pale sky.

Inside, the echoing grandeur of the ground floor surrounded them. The air was cool, tinged with old paper and furniture polish. Council workers passed by in swift bursts, their conversations muffled behind office doors. Sarah and Maureen moved with deliberate ease, feigning interest in historical plaques while scanning for the access point Art had identified.

It was on the second floor — an unmarked wooden door tucked behind a bulky filing cabinet in a quiet side corridor. A small brass plate read: **Authorised Personnel Only**.

Maureen spotted a nearby council worker — a harried man in a navy cardigan juggling a clipboard and a coffee. She stepped forward, calm and polite.

"Excuse me," she said. "My colleague and I are conducting a historical survey of Darwen's industrial heritage — a university project. We were hoping to document the Potts of Leeds clock mechanism. We've got permission from the Historical Society." She handed him the forged letter — complete with crests and signatures, carefully prepared by Art the night before.

The man squinted at it, then sighed. "I don't usually deal with this stuff…" He glanced down the corridor. "You'll need the tower key. It's in the caretaker's office — ground floor, past the service lift. Big blue door. Tell Frank I said it's fine. Just say Dave sent you."

"Thank you," Maureen replied quickly.

The blue door wasn't hard to find. Frank the caretaker grumbled but fetched the key without asking many questions. Sarah made light conversation about weather vanes while Maureen signed a visitor log under a false name. Moments later, they were back on the second floor, unlocking the narrow service door.

It creaked open, shutting out the buzz of the office behind them. Ahead: a narrow spiral staircase curling upward into silence. The air grew cooler, dustier, older.

They climbed. Each footstep echoed against the bare stone walls. As they rose, the rhythm of the clock's inner workings became clearer — a mechanical heartbeat, steady and unrelenting. It reverberated through their chests.

Eventually, the stairs opened into the belfry — a cavernous chamber of brass and shadow. Sarah's torch caught floating dust motes and towering gears. The Potts of Leeds mechanism loomed at the centre, gleaming brass cogs, groaning ropes, swinging pendulums. Five great bells hung high in the gloom — silent titans.

"Incredible," Sarah breathed, fear giving way to awe. "Those bells — John Warner & Sons. It's like standing inside the lungs of time."

Maureen raised an eyebrow. "Did you instinctively know that, or...?"

Sarah blinked.

Maureen pointed behind her. "You read the plaque."

Sarah grinned sheepishly. "Still counts."

They moved toward the clock's heart. The riddle echoed between them:

Three-two-four, the rhythm to reveal,
The final truth, the wounds to heal.

Sarah studied the large brass lever beneath the minute dial — worn smooth with use, clearly connected to the clock's hands outside. She frowned, tapping it gently.

"It has to be this," she murmured. "Part of the mechanism that moves the hands."

Maureen leaned closer. "You think the sequence refers to this?"

Sarah didn't answer immediately. She ran a finger along the edge of the cog housing, then glanced at the pendulum's slow, steady swing.

"Three-two-four," she repeated under her breath. "But... three what? Turns? Presses? Or something else?"

She reached for the lever, hesitated, then turned it cautiously — one notch, then two, then back again. The minute hand outside shifted slightly. No sound. No reaction.

"Maybe we're doing it backwards?" Maureen offered. "Two-three-four? Or are we meant to hold the turns?"

They tried again — another slow adjustment forward, this time starting with four notches. Still nothing. The clock ticked on, indifferent.

"This could take hours," Sarah muttered, frustration edging into her voice.

Then she paused, looking up at the brass inlays around the base of the central mechanism.

"Wait... it's not just the lever," she said slowly. "There are markings — like the compass rose. Different metals. Wear patterns."

Maureen crouched beside her. "So... we're not just turning time. We're selecting points. Like setting coordinates."

Sarah nodded, then tried again. This time, she moved the lever to the 'three' marker — a dull brass stud near the edge — then back two to a faintly scratched gear notch. Then forward again, to a fourth, larger disc set deeper into the mechanism's base.

She paused. "If this doesn't work—"

Click.

Then another.

Then, a deeper thrum — mechanical, ancient, like a buried engine stirring to life.

A panel to the right shuddered, then slid open with a slow, reluctant hiss.

Inside, nestled against faded velvet, sat a leather-bound book.

Heavy. Weathered. Unmistakably old.

Sarah reached in and lifted it free, her breath catching in her throat.

The Ainsworth Family Ledger.

Thick pages. Elegant handwriting. Not money. Not treasure. Something more powerful than both in Darwen: secrets.

Land deals. Hidden transactions. Property never formally recorded. The true map of a dynasty that had shaped the town from the shadows.

"This is it," Maureen whispered. "Leo was right."

But just as the truth settled over them, a new sound shattered the moment: a **clank** from below.

Footsteps.

Slow.

Measured.

Climbing.

A harsh white beam cut through the dust.

Elias Finch.

He had known. Not by chance, but because he'd walked the same path — studied the same secrets — only always a step behind. He didn't need to guess where they'd go next. He just had to wait.

His silhouette filled the stairwell, torch in one hand, brass-topped cane in the other. His composure was gone, replaced by something cold and furious.

His voice was low. Controlled. Deadly.

"Well, well," he said, stepping into the belfry. "The little historians have outdone themselves."

His eyes locked on the ledger in Sarah's hands. "Give it to me. It belongs to my family. To me."

He stepped forward, blocking the only exit.

Sarah clutched the book tighter. Maureen moved beside her, scanning for options.

But there were none.

They were trapped — caged in the heart of time, the bells looming above, the clock ticking behind, and **Finch** closing in.

CHAPTER THIRTEEN

The Chimes of Danger

Finch had found them.

His silhouette loomed at the top of the spiral stairs, brass-tipped cane in hand, eyes burning with predatory rage. The belfry vibrated with the relentless clunk of the clock as Sarah clutched the Ainsworth Ledger to her chest. Maureen stood in front of her, the only barrier between Finch and the truth he would kill to possess.

He stepped fully into the chamber, blocking their only exit. Behind him, the five bells hung like silent sentinels.

Sarah instinctively hugged the ledger tighter. Maureen's eyes swept the room, searching for anything they could use.

"This doesn't belong to you," Sarah said, her voice trembling but firm. "It belongs to Darwen. To the people. This ledger shows everything your family tried to bury."

Finch's lips curled. "Bury? You think this is some scandal? It's a testament. A record of legacy. Property, power, influence—never lost, only hidden. And now, it's mine to reclaim."

He took another step. "Give me the ledger, or I'll make sure you end up like your friend Leo. He's still alive—for now. But the cold, the dark, the silence... they wear a man down."

The words landed like a blow. Sarah's heart clenched at the image of Leo suffering somewhere in isolation. The ledger had once seemed like the end of their search. Now, it was clearly just the beginning.

"No," Maureen said sharply. "You're not getting this. And you're not going to hurt anyone else."

Finch's smirk vanished. He lunged—fast and brutal. The cane swung toward Sarah's shoulder.

Sarah ducked, stumbling back. Maureen stepped in, shoving a wooden gear lever into Finch's path, slowing him just enough.

"Give it to me!" Finch roared, his voice raw with rage.

Maureen's gaze snapped to the thick bell ropes beside her. Without hesitation, she seized one and yanked.

A deafening clang rang out as the nearest bell swung to life, its deep toll vibrating through stone and marrow. Finch staggered, hands clamped over his ears, momentarily stunned.

"Go!" Maureen shouted.

Sarah bolted for the stairs, Maureen close behind. The ledger pressed tight against her chest, its leather cover slick with sweat.

They thundered down the spiral stairwell, pursued by Finch's furious shouts and the erratic tap of his cane. Stone, dust, shadows. The clock ticked on, a pounding rhythm of urgency and peril.

They burst through the hidden second-floor door, nearly crashing into the same flustered council worker from before. He blinked in confusion as they raced past. Seconds later, Finch appeared, breathless and wild.

"Stop them! Thieves!"

The worker stood frozen as Sarah and Maureen tore through the grand corridors, dodging startled employees and baffled visitors.

"The north entrance!" Maureen gasped. "Service alley!"

They sprinted down a side hallway, past locked offices and faded noticeboards, until they reached the disused corridor Art had shown them on the blueprint. The walls narrowed around them, lined with cleaning supplies and old storage boxes. It reeked of damp paper and polish.

At the end, a heavy metal door. Maureen tried the handle.

"Locked," she muttered.

Sarah's eyes darted along the frame. "There—emergency release!"

Maureen threw her weight against the rusted bar. It groaned, then snapped free with a screech. The door flew open. Cold air rushed in.

They staggered into the alley, breathing hard. Finch's voice still echoed faintly behind them—but they didn't stop.

They ran. Past bins, past delivery vans, puddles splashing underfoot. They turned into the main street, disappearing into the bustle.

"We can't go to Art's," Sarah panted. "Finch'll be watching."

Maureen didn't argue. She scanned ahead and pointed. "Library. Public. Quiet corners. We vanish."

Darwen Public Library rose ahead—solid, safe, familiar. They slipped inside. Warmth and silence wrapped around them like a shield. The librarian at the desk offered a polite smile, unaware of the storm they'd escaped.

They headed straight for the local history section, tucking themselves into a secluded nook behind tall shelves. Only once they'd sat down did Sarah finally ease her grip on the ledger.

It lay in her lap—worn, ancient, and heavy with power.

The Ainsworth legacy. Exposed.

They had the truth now—but Leo's fate still hung in the balance. Finch had the means and the motive to act. The danger hadn't passed. Darwen's shadows still held secrets.

Maureen looked at Sarah. Her face was pale, but steady.

"We found the heart of the clock," she said softly. "Now we find Leo."

Sarah nodded. Her voice was barely a whisper.

"We end this. Together."

CHAPTER FOURTEEN

The Prisoner's Mark

The hushed sanctity of Darwen Public Library was a surreal contrast to the chaos Sarah and Maureen had just escaped. Tucked into a quiet corner of the local history section, partially hidden behind tall shelves of dusty tomes and fading records, they sat in silence, breath still ragged. The adrenaline was finally ebbing, leaving behind a trembling exhaustion.

Between them lay the Ainsworth Ledger — heavy, leather-bound, and monumental.

"We made it," Maureen whispered, her voice hoarse, eyes still wide with the aftershock.

Sarah nodded, her arms aching from clutching the ledger through the chase. But relief was fleeting. Finch's final words echoed in her mind:

He's still alive, for now — but his resolve is slipping. The cold, the dark, the silence... it wears a man down.

That wasn't just a threat — it was a clue. A cruel, vivid reminder. Wherever Leo was, he was suffering. And time was against them.

"We need to look through this," Sarah said urgently, sliding the ledger towards Maureen. "Fast. Finch called it his inheritance. If he's obsessed with it, then maybe it points to a place — somewhere private, connected to the Ainsworths — where he's keeping Leo."

They opened the book. The leather creaked softly. Inside, line after line of meticulous handwriting catalogued the Ainsworths' sprawling empire — property records, land transfers, cryptic notations. A hidden web of influence stretching across Darwen's history.

They flipped through page after page, scanning for anomalies: remote sites, unlisted addresses, old buildings buried in legal red tape.

"This is incredible," Maureen murmured, tracing a column of dense script. "It's like a shadow version of Darwen. One only they could see."

"But it doesn't help us find Leo," Sarah said, frustration mounting. "These are deeds, not directions. History, not hiding places."

The weight of it hit them. The ledger explained Finch's obsession, but it gave them nothing concrete about Leo. No coordinates. No direct leads. Just power — amassed, hidden, and inherited.

Sarah pulled out her phone. "I'm calling Art. He needs to know we're okay — and about Leo."

Maureen hesitated. "What if Finch traces it?"

"He's not MI5," Sarah said flatly. "Besides, we're not fugitives. Not officially. But if we go to the police without proof? Finch could spin it. Say we broke in. That we stole this." She tapped the ledger. "And while they're sorting that out, Leo could be moved. Or worse."

Maureen's face hardened. "Then it's down to us."

Sarah hit dial. Art answered on the second ring, his voice tight with worry.

"Sarah? Maureen? Are you alright? I saw Finch's van tear past here like a bat out of hell. I thought—"

"We're okay," Sarah cut in. "We've got the ledger. We're at the library — local history section. But Art… Finch has Leo. He told us. He's alive, but he's in a bad way."

There was a sharp intake of breath. "Leo's alive?" Art's voice cracked — relief, then fury. "That bastard. Of course he's using him as leverage. He won't let go until he gets what he wants."

"Art, listen. Do you remember the USB I used at the library?" Sarah asked.

"Still on my desk," he said immediately. "By the kettle."

"Leo loaded it with research — probably stuff Finch doesn't know about. Finch took his rucksack and notes, but not this. Can you check it? There might be something he overlooked."

"I'm on it," Art replied. They heard the faint clatter of drawers, then the hum of his old computer. "Okay... there's a folder: *Ainsworth Legacy – Anomalous Holdings*. Subfolders... wait. There's something odd."

Sarah and Maureen leaned in instinctively, the tension rising again.

"A utilities file," Art said. "Dated 2007. Mentions an *East Quarry Outbuilding – Shed D*. It's not on any modern maps. The note says the structure was flagged for unsafe access. Location: edge of Sandy Hollow, near the back trails. Council fenced it off years ago."

Sarah's pulse kicked up. "Would Leo have found that?"

"He must've come across it in the archives. But if it wasn't in the main registry, he might not have gone out there yet. Finch, with Leo's notes in hand, would've known exactly where to look."

Maureen's voice was low. "It's perfect. Abandoned. Isolated. No one would check. And Finch would see it as part of his inheritance."

"It's a match," Sarah said grimly. "That's where he's keeping him."

Art's voice grew urgent. "Then we don't have long. If Finch realises we've figured it out, he'll vanish. And he won't leave Leo behind."

They all knew what had to come next.

The puzzle was solved. The truth exposed. Now, they had to act.

A rescue.

Nightfall was only a few hours away. They'd move under cover of darkness — when Finch might be less alert. Art would dig up an old layout of Sandy Hollow. Maureen, ever prepared, still remembered enough first aid from her volunteer days. And Sarah — sharp, brave, and steady — would lead the way.

The ledger might serve as leverage, or a distraction, if it came to that.

From the tall library windows, Maureen spotted movement — a dark van cruising slowly down a side street. Engine low. Windows black.

"He's still out there," she murmured.

Sarah turned from the shelf, voice cold and calm. "Let him circle. We've got what he doesn't — and that gives us the edge."

They closed the Ainsworth Ledger, sealing its secrets again — for now.

Then, slipping quietly from the library and into the fading light of afternoon, they vanished once more into the streets of Darwen.

This wasn't about secrets anymore.

This was about saving Leo.

Before time ran out.

CHAPTER FIFTEEN

The Moor's Silent Watch

With one final, determined glance between them, Sarah and Maureen slipped out of Darwen Public Library. The low murmur of the building faded behind them, replaced by the hush of early evening — a stillness that made their urgent footsteps feel too loud. The Ainsworth Ledger was buried deep in Sarah's tote bag, its weight more than physical now. Leo was out there, and every second counted.

They moved quickly through back lanes, avoiding main roads. Finch would be watching — maybe not them directly, but for anyone who might interfere. Art had warned them not to return to the flat. He was right. But even stuck indoors, he was still helping.

Earlier, Art had texted a brief but precise message:

Behind bins in alley behind my flat. Waterproof bag. Everything you'll need. Be quick. Be quiet.

Ten minutes later, they reached the alley. Dusk had thickened, and the street lamps were slow to wake. Staying in the shadows, Maureen crouched behind the largest bin and pulled free a black plastic bag sealed tight with gaffer tape.

Inside: a high-powered torch, a compact crowbar, a small first-aid kit — and a decoy. A thick, leather-bound book nearly identical to the Ainsworth Ledger.

Sarah examined it in the dim light. "Looks like... a textile pattern book," she murmured, running a hand over the worn cover. "Perfect for fooling Finch in the dark — at least for a few seconds."

She slipped it into her bag beside the real ledger. A flicker of admiration crossed her face. Even from his flat, Art was always a step ahead.

They already had the location: **East Quarry Outbuilding — Shed D.** It had come from Leo's USB. Hidden, disused, fenced off by the council years ago. Officially unsafe. Practically forgotten.

Except by Finch.

They caught a bus to the edge of town, then began the long walk into Sandy Hollow — a stretch of dense woods spilling into open moorland. The trees pressed close, limbs tangled like knotted hands. The path beneath their boots was uneven, veined with roots and loose stone. The deeper they went, the quieter it became — no traffic, no lights. Just the crunch of twigs and the whisper of wind through undergrowth.

It took nearly an hour. By the time they reached the quarry's outer edge, night had fully fallen.

Shed D appeared like a shadow against the sky — sagging, weather-worn, half-swallowed by wild grass and moss. A rusted sign hung from the crooked fence:

UNSAFE STRUCTURE – KEEP OUT

But the padlock on the gate was new.

Maureen pointed to a clean break in the fence line. "That's fresh. Someone's been in recently."

"Finch," Sarah said quietly.

They slipped through the cut in the wire and crept towards the shed, torches off. The cold here was sharper. Still. As though the air itself was holding its breath.

Sarah eased the door open. It creaked, protesting the movement.

Inside was black as pitch. The smell hit first — mould, damp wood, rust... and something else. Something human. The cloying scent of someone left too long in one place.

They flicked the torch on, sweeping its beam slowly across the room. Broken crates. Collapsing shelves. A chain bolted to the wall. A single loop of iron dangling from the end.

Then — a cough. Low, dry, ragged.

Sarah froze. "Did you hear that?"

Maureen nodded. "Someone's here."

Another cough. Then a voice — hoarse, barely more than breath. "Who's there...?"

Sarah stepped forward, her voice soft. "It's okay. We're here to help."

A shuffling sound. Then a shape emerged — slumped against the back wall, partially obscured by debris. His hair was matted, his clothes grimy, but it was him.

Leo.

"Please... don't go..." he rasped.

Maureen was at his side in seconds, kneeling beside him. "You're safe now," she whispered. "We're getting you out."

Sarah took a step forward — and a sudden flash of white light exploded in her face.

She spun around — and froze.

"Well, well," came Finch's voice from the shadows. "Predictable. And so very disappointing."

He stepped fully into view, blocking the exit. The walking stick was in his hand again — brass-tipped, raised. His face was twisted in triumph. And something else: relief. As if this had always been the outcome he expected.

Sarah's heart thudded in her chest.

They'd found Leo.

But they'd walked straight into Finch's trap.

CHAPTER SIXTEEN

The Mill's Grasp

The blinding beam of Finch's tactical flashlight sliced through the damp dark, pinning Sarah and Maureen in its harsh glare. His face was twisted — a blend of fury and triumph — as he stepped forward, his voice low and guttural, echoing through the ruined shell of the outbuilding.

"I knew you wouldn't let it go," Finch growled, inching closer. "But I underestimated you. You didn't just stumble on this place... you've been using Leo's research, haven't you?"

He gestured toward Leo, slumped and shivering.

"That's how you found me. That's how you found him." His tone dripped with bitterness and accusation. "Well done. Now hand over the ledger."

The flashlight's beam shifted, landing on Leo's crumpled form. He lay against the back wall, chained by one wrist. His skin was ghostly, his hair matted with sweat and blood. A dark crust traced from his temple down his cheek. His eyes flickered open at the sound of Finch's voice — dazed, unfocused — then locked onto Sarah and Maureen. Recognition flared.

"You want the ledger?" Sarah said, her voice steadier than she felt. "Fine. Take it."

She reached into her bag, hand brushing past the real Ainsworth Ledger, gripping instead the decoy — the thick, leather-bound textile pattern book Art had prepared. Without hesitation, she yanked it free and hurled it.

The book struck Finch square on the temple with a satisfying thud. He let out a strangled cry, staggering sideways. The flashlight clattered to the floor, spinning wildly, its beam slicing across the mould-streaked walls.

"Now, Maureen!"

Maureen was already in motion. She grabbed the crowbar and swung it — not at Finch, but at a stack of rotting timber leaning precariously near the entrance. With a loud crack, the wood gave way, crashing across the shed floor in a heap, blocking Finch's advance.

Sarah darted to Leo's side. "We've got you," she whispered, inspecting the rusted chain shackling him to the wall.

Maureen joined her, pressing the crowbar into Sarah's hand.

"Brace yourself!" Sarah warned.

She jammed the bar into the padlock. With a grunt and a wrench of her shoulder, the old metal groaned — then snapped.

Leo slumped forward into her arms, weak but conscious.

"Who...?" he croaked.

"Friends," Maureen said, looping his other arm over her shoulder. "And we're getting you out."

Behind them, Finch roared: "You'll regret this!"

They didn't stop to look. Sarah guided them to a narrow crack in the wall — an escape route they'd spotted earlier. Beyond it lay the moor's edge: open, wild, and — they hoped — out of Finch's reach.

They spilled out into the cold night. The air hit like a slap. Wind ripped through the long grass, tugging at their clothes. Leo sagged between them, barely able to stand.

Sarah fumbled for her phone and called Art. "We've got him," she gasped. "He's alive — but he's in a bad way. We're on the moor. Finch is behind us."

Art's voice came through, tight with urgency. "Keep moving northeast. There are old outbuildings scattered across that stretch — stone stores, shepherd huts. Find cover. I'll get help."

Sarah relayed the instructions. The terrain was treacherous — sodden, uneven, pocked with pools of standing water. Every step was a battle. They dragged Leo through heather and marshy ground, breath fogging in the air, limbs aching.

Behind them, Finch's voice faded into the wind — but that didn't mean he'd stopped. Every gust could be his breath. Every broken branch, a step too close.

"We have to keep going," Maureen panted. "He's obsessed. He won't stop."

Sarah nodded, teeth clenched. "Then we disappear."

They weren't just running now.

They were surviving. They were fighting back.

CHAPTER SEVENTEEN

Sanctuary on the Moor

The moor stretched before them, vast and bleak under the indifferent gaze of the moon. Finch's furious shouts from the mill still echoed faintly in the distance, driving Sarah and Maureen forward across the treacherous terrain. Leo, barely conscious, sagged between them — a dead weight. His body shook uncontrollably, every breath a struggle, every step an agonising effort. Their lungs burned. Muscles screamed. But they didn't stop.

"This way!" Sarah panted, urging Maureen forward. Faint against the silver-lit horizon, she spotted the hunched silhouettes of low stone structures — just as Art had described.

They pressed on, the wind cutting into them like knives, biting through coats and skin. The moor offered no shelter — only gorse and heather that twisted into grotesque shadows. Behind them, Finch's footsteps still echoed. Steady. Relentless. He was closing in. Obsessed.

At last, a low, squat shape emerged from the dark — a crude stone shelter, little more than a pile of rocks with a collapsed roofline. A forgotten shepherd's hut. It looked like nothing. But to them, it was sanctuary.

"Here!" Maureen gasped, dragging Leo toward the doorway. Together, they half-carried, half-dragged him inside and collapsed onto the cold, earthen floor. The air was dank and heavy with the scent of mould, old straw, and sheep. But it was quiet. Hidden. For now, it was enough.

Maureen sprang into action, her old nursing instincts taking over. She tore open Art's bag, pulling out the first-aid kit. Leo was shaking violently, his skin icy and pale, the cut on his temple weeping at the edges.

"He's hypothermic and dehydrated," Maureen muttered, brow furrowed in concentration. She cleaned the wound, dressed it, and checked his breathing. Her movements were steady, efficient. "He needs warmth — and a doctor. Soon."

Sarah didn't hesitate. She stripped off her coat and wrapped it around Leo, rubbing his arms, trying to generate heat. "We can't go to A&E — not with Finch still out there."

Maureen nodded grimly, already pulling out her phone. "I know someone. Eleanor Vance. Retired GP. She taught me during my training. Still runs a private practice — quiet, discreet. She won't ask questions."

She dialled quickly, her fingers trembling with cold. "Eleanor? It's Maureen. I need help — urgent and off the record. Young man, head injury, hypothermic, possible concussion. We're on the moor, near Sandy Hollow."

A pause. Then relief washed over Maureen's face. "Thank you. I'll ping the location."

She hung up and sent the coordinates. Just as she tucked the phone away, the low growl of an engine rumbled across the moor.

Sarah tensed. "Finch. He's still looking."

Maureen crept to the doorway, peering through a crack in the stone. A pair of headlights sliced briefly across a distant hillside — then vanished. He was circling. Waiting. Hunting.

Inside, the cold closed in. Leo drifted in and out of consciousness, mumbling. Sarah crouched beside him and pulled the real Ainsworth Ledger from her bag. Its leather was cold, the weight heavy with meaning.

"We need to use this," she said softly. "It's the only leverage we've got. Finch still thinks we gave him the real one. If we lure him into the open — somewhere public — the police can take him."

Maureen nodded. "He'll realise the switch soon. That's when we act."

The minutes dragged. The wind moaned through cracks in the stone, rattling loose pebbles. They took turns keeping Leo warm, whispering to him, willing him to stay with them.

Then — a light. A slow, bobbing torch beam across the moor.

Sarah tensed again. Maureen gripped the crowbar.

But it wasn't Finch.

A lone figure emerged from the gloom — a woman in a long coat, a medical bag slung over her shoulder.

Dr. Eleanor Vance.

Relief broke through the tension like sunlight. Sarah nearly cried.

Without a word, Eleanor entered the hut and knelt beside Leo. Her expression was grave but calm. She checked his pulse, inspected the wound, then looked up at them.

"We'll stabilise him first," she said briskly. "Then you can tell me everything."

Sarah and Maureen exchanged a glance.

Leo was going to live.

But the storm they had walked into — Finch, the Ainsworth legacy, the lies buried beneath Darwen — hadn't passed.

And the next move would be theirs.

CHAPTER EIGHTEEN

Sanctuary and Recovery

The shepherd's hut had been a lifeline, but now it was behind them—just a stone shadow on the moor. They moved slowly under Eleanor Vance's steady guidance, the night stretching long and silent across the moorland as they carried Leo to safety.

He drifted in and out of consciousness during the journey, his murmurs incoherent, his body limp in their arms. They moved as a unit—Sarah and Maureen taking turns with the stretcher, Eleanor leading the way. The terrain was cruel: sodden trails, jagged dips, and tangled heather that snagged at every step. But the promise of shelter kept them going.

Eventually, the shimmer of distant streetlamps broke the horizon. Civilization. Eleanor's car waited at the moor's edge, hidden from passing eyes. They bundled Leo inside, layering him in every spare blanket they had. No words were exchanged—none were needed. They were past fear. Past panic. Now came resolve.

The drive was short, skimming the outskirts of Darwen in silence. Eleanor's clinic—disguised as a modest terraced house—was tucked behind a quiet row of trees, just far enough from town to avoid attention, but close enough to reach the centre quickly if needed. A forgotten outbuilding at the rear had been converted into a fully equipped private space.

Inside, it was everything they needed: warm, sterile, and calm. The sharp scent of antiseptic met them at the door. The hum of equipment gave the small space a comforting sense of order.

Eleanor wasted no time. With practiced ease, she transferred Leo to a private recovery room and connected him to monitors. The rhythmic beeping of the heart monitor was steady, grounding. Sarah and Maureen stood nearby, watching every movement, too exhausted to speak.

"He's stable," Eleanor said at last, removing her gloves. "The worst of the hypothermia is past. I've started him on fluids and antibiotics. He'll sleep for a while now. Let him."

Sarah nodded, swallowing the lump in her throat. She hadn't realised how tightly she'd been holding herself together.

In the quiet of the small waiting area, the fatigue finally hit. Sarah and Maureen slumped into chairs, the adrenaline that had carried them this far bleeding away. Their clothes were damp, boots caked in moorland mud, hands trembling with cold and tension.

"We did it," Sarah said softly, eyes on the floor.

Maureen didn't answer at first. She was staring down the corridor Leo had been wheeled through, her face unreadable. "He's alive," she said eventually. "But Finch is still out there."

Sarah reached into her bag and pulled out the real Ainsworth Ledger. It felt heavier now, the leather warped from damp and handling. She turned it in her hands like it was a live wire. "And Finch still thinks he has this."

Maureen's expression hardened. "Then we have a chance."

They sat in silence for a long while, the clinic's low hum the only sound. The weight of what they'd endured lingered in the air—exhaustion, relief, and the simmering knowledge that it wasn't over.

Outside, the wind swept past the windows, rattling the glass like distant footsteps.

The storm hadn't passed.

But Leo was safe.

And they were done running.

MILES DARBY

The next move would be theirs.

CHAPTER NINETEEN

The Final Gambit

While Sarah and Maureen found a fragile sanctuary for Leo, Elias Finch was consumed by a different kind of darkness. Having lost their trail on the moor, he retreated to the only place that gave him solace and control — his antique shop. But his fury hadn't cooled. It had crystallised.

He slammed the door behind him and stormed toward the counter, clutching the so-called ledger like a trophy. The leather felt right in his hand. The weight matched. But something — something — was wrong.

He flicked on the overhead light and dropped the book onto the counter.

He opened it.

His eyes scanned the pages.

Fabric designs.

Drawings.

Weaving notes.

No deeds. No names. No Ainsworth crest.

Not the ledger.

His face drained of colour. Page after page mocked him. His breath hitched as the truth formed.

They had fooled him.

A decoy.

He had been outplayed.

With a strangled cry, he hurled the book across the shop. It struck a wooden cabinet and fell to the floor with a heavy thud. He paced, fists clenched, chest heaving.

Then — the faint sound of something sliding across the floor.

He turned sharply.

A folded note had been pushed under the door.

He crossed the room in two strides, bent down, and picked it up. Cheap paper. Folded once. No name. Just a message:

We have what you want.
£10,000 — no games.
Come to your shop tomorrow at noon.
Alone. You'll get your ledger.

Finch stared at it.

Ten thousand pounds?

So that's what they were after. Not revenge. A deal.

He didn't smile — not quite. But his rage found new purpose.

This wasn't over.

Tomorrow, it would end.

At Eleanor's converted clinic just outside Darwen, Sarah and Maureen sat beside Leo. He was asleep now, stable, colour returning to his face. Between them, the real Ainsworth Ledger lay like a sleeping lion — full of teeth and secrets.

Sarah ran her hand across its worn cover.

"He'll know by now," Maureen murmured. "That it's not the real one."

Sarah nodded. "And that we know where to find him. Sliding that note under his door was enough. He wants the real thing.

Desperately."

"So he'll show up."

"Oh, he'll show up."

They'd already phoned Darwen CID. Sarah hadn't asked for anyone specific — just someone in charge. A calm voice had answered. DS Mallory. Sarah kept it careful, tactically vague: a missing researcher, an unstable antiques dealer, and an offer to capture everything — if someone was willing to listen.

Mallory had listened.

And agreed.

"We'll be there," she'd said. **"Quietly."**

Finch didn't sleep.

By morning, he was already pacing in the shop. A black zip case sat on the counter. Inside: £10,000 in cash. He'd made the withdrawal first thing, still seething. If that's what it took, he'd pay.

He just wanted the damn book.

The bell above the door jingled at exactly noon.

Sarah stepped in. Maureen followed.

No greetings. No small talk. Just quiet calculation on all sides.

Finch eyed the bag Sarah carried. "You've got it?"

"We've got it," she said calmly. "But before we hand anything over, you're going to tell us exactly what this is all about."

He scoffed. "I'm not playing your games."

"No games," Sarah replied. "Just answers. If you want the ledger, you'll give us the truth."

Finch hesitated. Then his gaze dropped — not in defeat, but calculation. He nodded once, almost to himself.

"You know what that book is?" he said. "It's not just records. It's not nostalgia. That ledger — the real one — proves that half of

Darwen isn't owned by who people *think* it is. The Ainsworths...
they were smart. And greedy. They bought up land under
different names, fake trusts, shell companies, even buried some
of it in church leases and foundations. Leaseholds disguised as
donations. Entire estates 'gifted' on paper — but still controlled by
the family. And when they started to die off, the trail went cold.
The paper trail vanished."

Sarah and Maureen stayed silent. He was warming up now — his
voice low and bitter.

"But the ledger didn't vanish," he went on. "It *tracks* every shell
name, every transfer, every payout. It shows exactly who profited
from every mill, every street corner. It connects the names that
were erased. There's money still moving — *today* — through trusts
that were set up over a hundred years ago. Quietly, quietly. With
no heirs. Because the real owners were never supposed to be
found."

He moved closer, eyes bright.

"But I found them. Or I would have — if Leo hadn't beaten me to it.
That rucksack of his had half the puzzle. He dug too deep, too fast.
I had no choice."

"You kidnapped him," Maureen said, her voice steady.

Finch waved that off like an inconvenience. "I just needed time.
Time to match the names. Time to piece the chain of ownership
together. You think this was about *legacy*?" He scoffed. "This was
about *control*. Power. That ledger holds the deeds to Darwen's real
wealth. Land. Infrastructure. Money that's still sitting, unclaimed,
because no one can trace it."

"And you wanted to claim it," Sarah said.

He met her eyes without blinking. "I *deserve* to claim it. My
grandfather was cut out. Left with nothing while the others
played kings. If the world had been fair, my name would be on half
those deeds. But it wasn't. So I corrected the course."

"And what would you have done if Leo had died in that shed?"

Maureen asked, her voice cold now.

Finch paused. "He didn't. He was never supposed to. I made sure he had food. Water. I just needed to slow him down. To finish what I started."

Sarah shook her head. "That's not justice, Mr. Finch. That's delusion."

Then — the door creaked open behind them.

Footsteps. Deliberate. Calm.

A woman stepped inside. Plainclothes. Badge clipped to her belt.

"I'm Detective Sergeant Mallory, Darwen CID," she said clearly. "And we've heard everything, Mr. Finch."

He turned slowly, face paling.

"You—what?"

"We've had a live feed since you started talking," she said. "You've just confessed to unlawful imprisonment, obstruction, and conspiracy to conceal historical property fraud — possibly attempted murder. You've been very helpful."

She nodded to the uniformed officer at the door.

"Mr. Finch, you're under arrest."

He stood stunned — not shouting, not resisting. Just stunned. The truth he'd been chasing had buried him instead.

CHAPTER TWENTY

The Unravelling Thread

A week had passed since that dawn showdown in Darwen Town Square. Elias Finch now sat in police custody, his furious claims about stolen legacies confined to the sterile walls of an interview room. The decoy ledger — the old textile pattern book Art had selected — rested quietly in an evidence locker, tagged and catalogued as if it were the true prize. But the real Ainsworth Ledger had never been mentioned in the official reports.

Sarah had slipped it back into Art's flat, hidden in plain sight. Wrapped in a faded dust jacket and tucked between towers of railway timetables and forgotten auction catalogues, it now lay silent among the clutter, waiting. They'd agreed: what the book contained was too dangerous to hand over blindly. For now, secrecy was safety.

Leo Davies, under Dr. Eleanor Vance's watchful care, had begun to recover. The tremors had eased. The bruises faded. And though the haunted look hadn't entirely left his eyes, the old spark — that sharp, insatiable curiosity — had returned. He was still weak, but he'd asked to see Art.

The invitation came as soon as Eleanor deemed him strong enough. It felt right — a return to the place where the pieces had first started to fit together.

Art's flat was unchanged. Still a museum of maps, yellowing receipts, and curios piled in teetering stacks. And yet, as Leo stepped carefully through the door, leaning slightly on Maureen's arm, the chaos felt comforting. Familiar.

Art extended a hand. "Leo Davies, I presume? Art Ainsworth — though I daresay I feel like I know you already. The Rucksack Lad, in the flesh."

Leo gave a tired smile. "Thanks... all of you. I don't remember much after Finch—after he cornered me. Just flashes. The mill. Chains. And then you two." He looked at Sarah and Maureen. "Who are you? How did you even know I was there?"

Sarah leaned forward. "When we started looking for you, it felt like a treasure hunt — except the treasure was you. And the truth."

Leo blinked, surprised. She continued. "We followed your trail exactly. From the Blackwood Mill to the cylinder you found, then to Darwen Tower, and finally to the Town Hall clock tower."

She stood up and crossed the room to one of Art's overstuffed bookcases. "You left more than clues behind," she added.

She reached between two faded railway timetables, pulled aside a curling auction catalogue, and eased out a worn, cloth-wrapped volume tucked deep in the shelf. She unwrapped the faded dust jacket with care, revealing aged leather beneath — cracked, but unmistakably deliberate.

She returned and set the book down on the coffee table with a quiet thud.

The Ainsworth Ledger.

Sarah tapped the cover. "And that's where we found this. Everything you suspected — the buried ownership, the land, the trusts — it's all in here."

Leo's gaze lingered on the ledger, his voice hushed. "You actually followed it all..."

"Every step," Maureen said softly. "And we didn't stop until we found you."

Leo settled into Art's most battered armchair, a steaming mug of tea in hand. The real Ainsworth Ledger rested between them like a sleeping lion. They took turns piecing together the story — not just the rescue, but everything that had led them there.

"It started with a name," Leo explained, voice steadier now. "I was researching post-industrial land use — how towns like Darwen adapted after the mills shut down. But I kept hitting anomalies. Properties listed under shell names... fragments tracing back to old textile holdings. The name 'Ainsworth' kept popping up. Again and again."

He drew a slow breath. "What really caught my eye was how many sites quietly changed hands — or never appeared on public record at all. It looked like a second Ainsworth empire. Hidden from taxes, scrutiny, the lot. When I found mentions of a ledger — a single volume detailing the whole thing — I knew I had to keep going."

"And that's when Finch found you," Maureen said.

Leo nodded. "He came to one of my uni talks. Didn't speak. Just watched. Then I saw him again outside the local archives. He must've been tracking my progress."

Art tilted his head. "So you went to him?"

"I did. I thought he might have old records or family links. And I'd seen something in his shop window — an heirloom box that matched sketches from the Ainsworth family archive. When he approached me outside the market, he seemed helpful. Said he had material that could help."

He paused, then added, "At first, I was careful. But then I pulled out my notebook to show him a reference, and I think the corner of the cylinder was showing in my bag. That changed everything."

"He recognised it," Sarah murmured.

Leo nodded grimly. "He'd heard of it, maybe seen drawings. But the moment he saw the real thing, he knew. And he knew I'd found more than rumours — I had proof. He blocked the door. Said it was his family's. That I'd stolen it. When I didn't give it up, he snapped."

86

Silence followed.

Art finally said, "That cylinder led us to the hidden mechanism in the Town Hall tower. Then to the ledger. You were right, Leo — all of it. Finch wasn't just chasing family secrets. He wanted to rewrite history — put himself at the centre of it."

"And destroy anyone who stood in his way," Sarah added.

Leo looked down at his mug. "So what now? With the ledger? With everything?"

"We're still figuring that out," Maureen said. "You uncovered a truth the town deserves to know. But it needs to be handled carefully."

Sarah nodded. "We can't just dump it all online. There'll be land disputes. Legal chaos. Political fallout. We need a plan. Maybe even create a trust — something to manage the land properly, fund local projects, preserve what matters."

Art chuckled. "The Ainsworth Trust for Darwen — poetic, really."

Leo smiled faintly. "I came here to study history. Never thought I'd become part of it."

Sarah's eyes were soft but firm. "You didn't just become part of it, Leo. You changed it."

They raised their mugs — to survival, to truth, to the threads finally beginning to stitch back together.

Outside, Darwen bustled on, unaware of how close its past had come to swallowing its future.

Inside, the real ledger lay open beneath the lamplight.

Leo idly skimmed the final pages — mostly blank. But something caught his eye. A smudge. Not ink. Indentations. Faint marks.

He tilted the page toward the light.

Dots. Dashes. A pattern. A code.

Sarah noticed. "Leo?"

He didn't answer at first, his fingers tracing the indentations. Then, quietly: "This isn't over. There's something else. A cipher."

Art leaned closer. "You're sure?"

Leo nodded. "It was left for someone to find. Not easily. But deliberately."

Maureen folded her arms. "So it's not just a ledger. It's a map."

Sarah gave a stunned laugh. "We've only scratched the surface."

Leo closed the book carefully, his expression lit with something fresh — purpose.

"We're not done yet."

A NOTE TO THE READER

Thank you for reading *Darwen's Echoes: The Mill's Grasp*. If it kept you up at night, made you curious about your own town's secrets, or left you looking at derelict buildings a little differently - then it's done its job.

Please consider leaving a review on Amazon. It only takes a moment, and it helps indie authors like me more than you know.

Want to find out what's next?
Follow me on Facebook.

ABOUT THE AUTHOR

Miles Darby

A Northern writer fascinated by faded maps, industrial ghosts, and the unspoken truths that linger in old buildings. He blends contemporary mystery with buried histories and believes every town has its own secrets worth unearthing.

Darwen's Echoes: The Mill's Grasp is his debut novel.

COMING SOON

Darwen's Echoes - The Hidden Estate

Just when they thought the truth was within their
grasp, Leo, Sarah, Art, and Maureen uncover a
chilling secret in the heart of the Ainsworth Ledger:
a cryptic cipher leading to a vast, hidden fortune.

As they race to unravel clues woven into ancient textiles
and etched into the very landscape of Darwen's past,
they disturb a powerful, unseen enemy - those who have
illegally profited from generations of concealed wealth.

The game has changed. The stakes are higher.

And Darwen's deepest secrets are about
to be unearthed, for good or ill.

Printed in Dunstable, United Kingdom

68577229R00057